BLIND SIDE

They drew level with the stone box and peered inside. There was an instant of stunned silence, then Frankie turned and ran back down the slope. Alice gasped and clapped both hands over her mouth, and David shook his head slowly from side to side as though he could not accept what he was seeing. Michael was the only one who did not react with shock. He felt nothing but a tired recognition as he gazed at the small, dried-up body squatting inside the box.

'Oh, the poor thing,' said Alice, her voice trembling with sadness. 'It's a little girl, isn't it?'

Ann Coburn

BLIND SIDE

RED FOX

A Red Fox Book

Published by Random House Children's Books
20 Vauxhall Bridge Road, London SW1V 2SA

A division of The Random House Group Ltd
London Melbourne Sydney Auckland
Johannesburg and agencies throughout the world

First published in Great Britain by Red Fox 2001

Printed and bound in Denmark by Norhaven

Papers used by The Random House Group Ltd are natural, recyclable
products made from wood grown in sustainable forests.
The manufacturing processes conform to the environmental
regulations of the country of origin.

THE RANDOM HOUSE GROUP Limited Reg. No. 954009

www.randomhouse.co.uk

ISBN 0 09 940079 0

For Hazel, my twin sister.
Born together. Always together.

'The thing on the wrong side of the door,
On the blind side of the heart.'

G. K. Chesterton
Ballad of the White Horse

1

Michael takes a while to get the full picture. He comes round slowly, floating up through fathoms of sleep like a diver returning to the surface. *Hot*, is his first thought. *Too hot*. Somewhere above him, his body is burning up but all he wants to do is dive back down into sleep again. He tries, but an irritating pain will not stop hammering at his bones. Michael frowns and the skin of his forehead tears apart like tissue paper.

What . . .? Suddenly Michael is desperate to wake up. *What . . . ?* He struggles to open his eyes but sinks down into sleep again and is lost.

The slope of the sand dune looked innocent enough, smooth and soft and white, but Alice inspected it suspiciously before she sat down. She was wearing a new school skirt and was trying very hard to keep it clean. The odds were stacked against her. Things just seemed to happen to Alice's clothes. Her last school skirt had disintegrated after an accident in the science lab and the one before that had never recovered from their Local Studies field trip to the sewage works.

Carefully, Alice lowered herself onto the sand and straightened the skirt over her long legs. No rips, no stains, not even a crease. Satisfied, she leaned back on her hands and started scanning the beach for David, Frankie and Michael, her three best friends. They were going to be difficult to spot. It was the last afternoon of the summer term and the teachers had marched everyone down to Philadelphia Bay for the traditional end-of-year barbecue. The whole stretch of the beach, from the tide line to the dunes, was littered with figures dressed in blue and grey school uniform. A long line of boys danced at the edge of the sea with their trousers rolled up to their knees, jumping waves. Alice scanned the line, searching for David's distinctive, sun-bleached hair, but there was no sign of him.

She turned her attention to a mixed group clustered at the base of the biggest dune. Someone had found a sheet of plastic on the beach and they were taking turns to sand-surf down the steep slope. Alice studied the spectators, expecting to find Michael on the edge of the group, quietly watching the action as he always did, but she drew a blank.

A thin cheer rose from the crowd as one surfer made it all the way to the bottom, finishing off with a spectacular spray of sand. Alice smiled. *That's got to be Frankie*, she thought as the spectators surged forward to surround the champion. But it was Nigel Dunn, not Frankie, who emerged from the scrum. He saw Alice watching and shook his clasped hands above his head. Alice assumed a bored expression and turned away.

Where were they? Surely they hadn't gone off somewhere without her, not today? It was their last school day as a foursome. In a few weeks' time,

Frankie would be on a plane, flying back to California.

Alice scowled. She had been feeling prickly and out-of-sorts all afternoon. Now she felt abandoned too. She blinked fiercely a few times, then bent her head and let her long black hair fall forward over her face. It was dim and cool in the hair cave. Peaceful. She decided to stay for a while, watching fragments of sunlight as they filtered between strands of hair and fluttered across her school skirt.

'Geronimo!'

Something slammed into Alice's back and sent her sliding and rolling down the face of the dune. She came to a halt on the beach and sat up, spitting sand. Frankie was doing a log roll down the dune right behind her.

'The skirt. Watch the skirt!' yelped Alice. She shot her hands out behind her and scuttled sideways out of Frankie's way like a crab, lifting her backside clear of a patch of slimy seaweed as she went.

'Gotcha!' crowed Frankie, clambering to her feet and staggering in a dizzy circle. 'I've been stalking you for ages and you didn't know a thing about it.'

'I knew you were there.'

Frankie hooted disbelievingly.

'I did! I just pretended not to notice.'

'Yeah, yeah.' Frankie mimed pulling a knife from its sheath. 'I could've slit your throat from ear to ear.' She gave Alice an evil grin, then leaned forward and shook a load of damp sand out of her tight, black curls.

'Hey! I said watch the skirt!' yelled Alice.

'Hey! Enough about the skirt!' Frankie yelled

right back. She glared down at Alice for a few seconds, then suddenly deflated and slumped onto the sand beside her. 'Dumbest thing I ever heard – making us wear school uniform to the beach.'

'We always wear uniform on school outings.'

'Oh, puh-leeze! Shirts and ties? On the beach? Only in Britain.'

'It's traditional,' muttered Alice, feeling quaint and silly.

'Whatever. I don't care. A few more weeks and I'm outta here. Boy, will I be glad to go.' Frankie gave Alice a brisk nod to emphasise how glad she would be. 'Yup. Can't wait. Adios Dullsville,' she added, turning to wave at the place which had been her home for the past ten months. 'Goodbye—'

Frankie lowered her hand. There was a silence as they both gazed past the far end of the bay to the town. It made a beautiful picture. Sandstone houses jostled for space around the little harbour, their red roofs bright in the sunshine. Two long rowing boats glided under the striding arches of the Royal Border Bridge while, high above them, a train soared out across the river. Alice waited until the whole length of the train had crossed the bridge before she spoke.

'Frankie?' she said softly.

Frankie blinked and picked up where she had left off. '—Goodbye Grunge Town. Yup, the minute my dad's contract is up, I'm gone. No more soggy chips. No more treacly tea. No more freezing my tail off on the hockey pitch. No more gale force winds blowing through my bedroom. You know, you guys really should come round to the idea of properly fitted windows . . .'

4

Frankie came to a halt and set her mouth in a hard line to stop the trembling in her lip. Wordlessly, Alice reached out and hugged her. Frankie allowed her head to tilt until it rested lightly on Alice's shoulder.

'Want to come to my house for tea?' asked Alice, after a few moments.

Frankie shrugged.

'You can do a make-over if you like,' offered Alice, selflessly. She knew Frankie would not be able to resist. 'Make-up . . . Clothes . . . as bright as you want . . .'

'Hair too,' demanded Frankie, twisting round and giving Alice an assessing look.

'All right,' said Alice, reluctantly.

'Can I cut it?'

'No!'

'Just a smidgeon—'

'Where can David and Michael be?' said Alice, looking for a change of subject.

Frankie delivered one of her trademark, evil grins. 'I don't know about Michael,' she said. 'But I'll bet you one haircut I can lead you straight to Davey-boy.'

Michael is surfacing again. The first thing he knows is fear. Something dreadful is floating just above him, waiting for him to remember.

Skin . . . he thinks. The word acts like a key, unlocking his memory. Suddenly the dreadful thing is upon him. He comes awake in one horrified lurch, remembering how the skin of his forehead tore apart like tissue paper. He tries to lift his hand to his head but stops as pain shoots along his arm. The pain spreads through his body and Michael realises he is curled up as tight as a jack-in-a-box. His muscles are knotting with cramp but his bones ache too much to try unfolding.

I must be very ill, he thinks. Then, *Dad . . . Call Dad . . .* Michael hesitates. He and his dad aren't talking much these days. *Emergency, stupid. Call Dad!* He tries to take a breath and chokes on a mouthful of gravel.

Gravel . . .? Even as his body struggles to find some air, his mind is grappling with a terrifying new idea. He is not curled up in his own bed. He is – *where . . .?* Fragments of information explode like fireworks in his oxygen-starved brain.

Not gravel, he thinks as he opens his mouth wide and tries to push the stuff out with his tongue. *Not gravel . . . Salt . . .* His mouth is crusted with big, rough crystals of salt. He can taste it.

Michael gives up on clearing his mouth and tries sucking air in through his nostrils. It is stale and hot and dry, with precious little oxygen, but it clears his head enough to realise that he is not lying down at all. He is upright, squatting on his haunches with his legs drawn up to his chest and his knees digging into the soft place under his chin. There is a wall of stone at his back and he is crouched on a pile of salt crystals.

Where am I?

His eyelids feel as though they have been glued together over a thin layer of sand but he forces them open, ignoring the pain as they tear apart and scrape back into the sockets. There is nothing to see. He is in a dark place without the slightest glimmer of light.

Gritting his teeth against the cramp in his neck, Michael tries to lift his chin from his knees. The back of his head slams into something hard and the shock jerks his arms out sideways. His elbows grate against rock and there is a tearing pain as the skin peels away from the bone. Michael pulls his arms back to his sides and sits motionless for a few seconds, fighting back a rising surge of panic. He pulls the hot, stale air into his lungs, trying to find enough oxygen to keep his head clear, then carefully worms one hand up the side of his body to feel above his head. A roof of stone hangs centimetres away from the back of his neck.

His mind is beginning to blur but he makes one last effort to think. There is solid stone at his back, above his head and on each side. The only possibility of escape is straight ahead. He clenches his jaw, then inches his hands out into the darkness. Almost immediately, his fingers graze against a wall of rock. Michael lets out a small whimper of fear. He has no idea how he came to be here, squeezed and folded into a box of stone so small he can barely move, but he is sure of one thing.

He is trapped.

As he begins to lose consciousness, Michael tries to scream, but the air is all gone.

'Toldya,' whispered Frankie, parting a tussock of marram grass for Alice to view the scene below them.

Alice shuffled forward through the sand,

commando-style, to lie on her belly beside Frankie at the top of the dune. Directly below them was the sheltered hollow behind the beach where the barbecue had been set up. Two hours earlier the hollow had been packed with people queueing for food or eating with their friends. Now only the teachers remained, filling black sacks with plastic cups and half-eaten burger buns. Alice peered more closely at the couple who were hauling rubbish sacks from the hollow up to the mini-bus in the car park. One was their new form tutor, Miss Broadbent, and the other was David.

Frankie snipped the air with an imaginary pair of scissors. 'You owe me one hair cut.'

Alice did not answer. She was busy scowling down at David and their new form tutor. The trouble was that Miss Broadbent was neither broad nor bent. She was slim and straight and lovely. She had huge, soft, toffee-coloured eyes. Her hair fell in buttery curls down to her shoulders, which curved out of her sleeveless summer dress, as smooth and brown as a pair of speckled eggs. Since her arrival at the start of the summer term, all the boys had been spellbound. It made no difference to them that Miss Broadbent shared a flat with James Nardini, the new museum curator. They were content simply to worship her, David included. As Alice watched him struggle up the slope to the car park, dragging Miss Broadbent's sack as well as his own, she felt an uncharacteristic twinge of jealousy.

'Earth to Alice,' roared Frankie, right next to her ear. 'Do you read me? I said, you owe me one hair cut.'

'You're not coming near my hair with a pair of scissors,' hissed Alice.

Frankie sat up, looking very offended. 'I kept my part of the deal. I led you straight to Davey-boy.'

Alice sat up too. 'I never agreed to that deal! Anyway, it didn't take a genius to guess where he'd be.'

'Oops,' said Frankie, gazing over Alice's shoulder. 'We've been rumbled.'

Alice turned to look. David and Miss Broadbent had stopped halfway between the hollow and the car park. The teacher was waving up at them excitedly and pointing down at something in the rough grass at her feet.

'Come and see, girls!' called Miss Broadbent. 'And you, boys!' she added, spotting a group of boys who had sneaked back to sniff out any left-overs.

Alice and Frankie shared a look, then clambered to their feet and headed down the slope. As Alice plodded after Frankie, the spiky irritation that had been hovering over her all afternoon settled on her shoulders and dug in its claws.

'This is so exciting!' called Miss Broadbent as they approached. 'Guess what David found!'

'His brains in a bag?' muttered Alice, taking in the soppy grin on David's face. Frankie sniggered beside her. They struggled on over the tussocky grass and reached the teacher at the same time as the boys.

'What is it, Miss?' said Nigel Dunn in a bright, ready-to-learn voice which made Frankie snigger again. Nigel threw her a look of pure hate then rearranged his face into a smile and turned back to Miss Broadbent.

'It's the remains of the lost village of Philadelphia!' gasped Miss Broadbent. Alice winced at the enthusiasm in the teacher's voice. Why did she always have to talk in exclamation marks?

'We know, Miss,' said Alice.

'Really, Miss?' said Nigel, at exactly the same time, drowning Alice out. She rolled her eyes in exasperation. Nigel knew about the village; they all did. It had been part of their Local Studies course.

Miss Broadbent beamed at Nigel. 'Come and see! Look! Here! A doorstep!' She bent and cleared the grass from a flat stone at her feet. 'And over there, that lumpy mound covered in nettles, that's a wall!'

'Fascinating,' drawled Alice.

'Isn't it? Once you know what you're looking for, you can see the site of each cottage – and this flatter bit running through the middle must be the main street!'

'The only street, Miss,' offered Nigel. 'It was a tiny village – homes for the lime workers.'

'Really?' Miss Broadbent turned to Nigel, her face shining with interest.

'Yes,' countered David. 'That's why the land around here has so many dips and hollows, see?' Miss Broadbent rewarded him by turning her shining face his way. Gratified, he continued. 'It's where they quarried the limestone.'

Nigel jumped in. '—and you see those funny-shaped stone efforts over there, built into the cliff side, Miss? Those are the kilns where they heated up the limestone and turned it into quicklime. They used it for building before cement. That's why the village died, Miss. When cement came along, we didn't need quicklime any more.'

As the contest for Miss Broadbent's attention continued, Alice and Frankie watched with growing disbelief. Anyone in their right mind could see what was happening. History was Miss Broadbent's specialist subject. She was only pretending to be ignorant to find out how much they knew. Frankie waited for David to look her way, then opened her mouth and pretended to stick two fingers down her throat. David put on his tolerant, mature expression and Frankie narrowed her eyes at him, like a cat.

'Grow up,' mouthed David and turned back to Miss Broadbent.

'Did you know, Miss,' said Nigel, 'that they found some severed heads when they were quarrying?'

'That's just a story,' said David.

'No! Really?' said Miss Broadbent, giving Nigel her full attention.

'Really. In an airtight oak box, preserved in cedar oil.'

'That's just a stupid story,' insisted David, but Nigel talked over him.

'People say they were the heads of Celtic warriors, taken in battle. And there was gold in the box, too. Some of those funny, twisty necklaces they used to wear.'

'It's not true!' yelled David. 'If they'd found something like that it would be in the museum!'

'Boys, boys,' gurgled Miss Broadbent. 'Don't fight! David may well be right, Nigel. You often get these old fables about places where there's supposed to be hidden treasure. They're good fun but – only stories.'

Nigel scowled and Miss Broadbent hurried to soothe his hurt feelings. 'But it was a very interesting story, Nigel. Can you remember the proper name for those funny, twisty necklaces?'

'Um . . . chokers?' guessed Nigel and was rewarded with a snigger from Frankie.

'I know what we need,' said Miss Broadbent, suddenly.

'What?' said David and Nigel together, both poised to run and fetch whatever she wanted.

'An expert. We need Michael. He's so good at history. He'd be able to tell us the proper name for those neck rings. Where do you think he is?'

David had a sudden, fierce desire to be Michael. It was a strange feeling. He had never wanted to be anyone other than his own self. He folded his arms and scowled at the ground.

'Alice? Could you go and find Michael?'

'I'll go, but if you'd asked me, I could've told you,' said Alice. 'They're called torcs.'

She turned on her heel and marched off but the feeling of triumph did not last long. *Why is it always me?* she thought, as she trudged steadily up the side of a dune on the far side of the hollow. *Because I lie down and let them walk all over me, that's why. No-one would dream of asking Frankie. She'd wipe the floor with them.*

Alice blew the hair out of her face and cast a resentful glance back at the others. They were all lounging on the sand, talking and laughing, with Miss Broadbent at the centre of the group.

'Alice,' she mimicked. 'Go and find Michael while the rest of us stay here and sunbathe.' Alice glowered at Miss Broadbent then turned back to the task of climbing up the dune. The sun beat down on the top of her head, her shoes filled up with sand and her irritation grew as she remembered what she would be doing in two days' time.

'Alice, you won't mind helping me with the twins' birthday party on Sunday, will you? You won't mind giving up your whole day to play party games on the beach with ten completely mad eight year olds, will you?' 'No, Mum, I'd be happy to trail around after my horrible brothers. No, of course I didn't have any plans of my own . . .'

Panting, Alice reached the top of the dune and looked down the other side. What she saw there pushed all complaints out of her head. For a second she stood frozen, then her heart gave a shocked lurch and the blood pounded in her ears. She filled her lungs and shrieked at the top of her voice.

'Miss!'

It was only one word but it arced across the clear blue sky like a distress flare. Down in the hollow, the whole group span round and looked up at her. Miss Broadbent's toffee-coloured eyes widened as she saw the fear on Alice's face.

'Miss!' called Alice, a second time. Then she turned, plunged down the other side of the dune and disappeared.

2

'Stay here, all of you,' ordered Miss Broadbent over her shoulder, already running after Alice.

David and Frankie looked at one another, nodded, then set off after Miss Broadbent, shoulder to shoulder.

'She said to stay!' called Nigel. He watched their steadily retreating backs for a few seconds, then shrugged and followed at a trot, with the rest of the boys trailing behind him.

Alice flung herself down the dune slope, taking giant steps. She built up such a speed, her legs could not keep up and she somersaulted down the last few yards. At the bottom, she bounced up onto her feet again and continued running, spitting sand. She followed the curve of the dune, heading for the spot where Michael's body rested. Body was the right word. There was an emptiness about it, an absence of life, which had been horribly obvious even as she looked down from the top of the dune.

'Please be all right, please be all right...' she intoned as she raced across the sand towards him, but the closer she got, the worse the picture grew. Michael was curled up like a baby, lying on his side against the slope of the dune. He was completely still. One side of his face was buried in the sand and the other side – Alice felt her stomach clench and her mouth fill with a coppery taste as she saw the other side. His mouth was hanging slackly open and his lips were a dull, bruised purple. There were blue smudges down the side of his nose and under his eye. The rest of his face was grey.

'Michael,' gasped Alice, dropping to her knees beside him. What to do? She brushed the hair from his forehead and laid her hand against his cheek. The skin was cold and clammy.

'Come on, Michael. Please . . .' She lifted his eyelid and then wished she hadn't. His eye had rolled so far back into his head that only the white was showing. Alice hesitated, not sure whether she should try to move him. She dug her hands into the dune on each side of his head and tried to lift his face clear of the sand but his whole body was rigid, frozen into its strangely cramped pose.

Alice shifted position, placed her hands under Michael's knees and pushed until he rolled onto his back, still curled up with his hands clasped around his shins. His face came out of the dune, but all the sand which had collected in the buried side of his mouth now slid in a wet lump to the back of his throat.

'Stupid! Stupid!' sobbed Alice, wrenching him onto his side again. She dug her fingers into his mouth, pulling out as much sand as she could, then she put her ear to his lips. There were no breath sounds and no air tickled her cheek.

'Come on, Michael,' she crooned, patting his face. There was no response.

'Come on. Wake up,' she said more loudly, the

pats turning into slaps. Still, Michael gave no sign of life.

Alice put her mouth right next to his ear and shouted, 'Michael!' He did not even flinch. She looked over her shoulder but Miss Broadbent was nowhere in sight. Desperately Alice trawled through her patchy knowledge of first aid.

'O.K. His airway's clear. He's in the recovery position, sort of. But he's not breathing. He's not breathing . . .! He's not—'

Alice made herself calm down. She prised Michael's wrist away from his shin until she could slip her fingers into the gap. She tried to find a pulse but her own heart was beating too hard and fast to be sure of what she was feeling. She pulled her hand away and covered her face. How long before lack of oxygen caused brain damage?

Swiping her tears away, Alice leaned forward, pinched Michael's nostrils together and tried to give him mouth-to-mouth. There was no room. His knees were pulled up to his chin and held there in the vice-like grip of his arms.

'I'm trying to help you!' she yelled, suddenly angry. 'Stop scaring me!' She kneeled over him, clenched her hands together, locked her arms straight at the elbows and swung them up, then down again like a sledge hammer. Her fists thumped him hard between the shoulder blades and suddenly everything happened at once. His eyes flew open, his back arched and, as his chest uncurled, he made a dreadful grating noise in his throat, like a chain dragging across concrete.

'Alice!' shouted Miss Broadbent behind her. 'What on earth are you doing?'

Alice took no notice. She kneeled next to Michael and watched as he took a second breath, then a third. She saw the colour coming back to his face and slumped back on her heels, weak with relief. Miss Broadbent skidded to a stop beside her.

'I said what on earth are you doing, hitting him like that?'

Michael rolled over onto his front, propped himself up on his elbows and began coughing up sand. The teacher folded her arms and frowned down at Alice.

'Alice, there is no excuse for fighting! Look at him! You've knocked all the breath out of him!'

'I didn't, Miss! I was trying to make him breathe again. He was all blue. He was unconscious.'

'Blue?' The teacher kneeled down beside Alice. 'Are you sure?'

Alice nodded. Miss Broadbent studied Michael. He had finished coughing up sand and was lying face down with his head resting on his arms.

'Michael?' Miss Broadbent laid her hand on his back, feeling the rise and fall of his breathing. She moved her hand to his shoulder and shook it, gently. Michael erupted from the sand. His elbow connected solidly with Miss Broadbent's eye, knocking her backwards. Alice gasped and covered her mouth with her hand but Michael did not seem to realise what he had done. His eyes were wide and blank and full of fear. He turned his back on them and started digging furiously, hand over hand, down into the patch of sand where he had curled so still and lifeless just a few minutes earlier.

Frankie, David, Nigel and the other boys reached the top of the dune and spread out around the rim as they took in the scene below them. Miss Broadbent was sprawled on her back clutching her face, a tearful Alice was trying to pull her to her feet and Michael – Michael was tunnelling down into the sand like a starving dog digging for a bone. It should have been comical, but there was an intensity about his actions that reduced them all to an uneasy silence.

Frankie shot David one questioning look then turned away, folding her arms. She was trying to look casual but David saw how her fingers were digging into her elbows.

'It'll be all right,' he said, lightly, shoving his hands into his pockets before clenching them into fists. 'He'll be in a state about nothing. You know him.'

'Crazy as a coot,' said Frankie in the same light tone, frowning down at Michael.

'Mad as a hatter,' agreed David.

'Should be put away,' sneered a voice on David's other side. Together they turned to face Nigel Dunn.

'What did you say?' said David, with a dangerous pleasantness.

'Looney Tunes,' said Nigel, pointing down at Michael, then using the same finger to draw little circles at his temple.

Without warning, Frankie launched herself at Nigel and head-butted him in the chest. He fell down the slope in a slow, undignified somersault.

Coins cascaded from his pockets and disappeared into the sand. He came upright again halfway down the slope and turned, planting his feet wide apart for balance. Frankie stared down at him, secretly shocked at what she had done. She had been feeling grouchy all afternoon but that blast of anger had come out of nowhere.

'What the hell was that for?' spluttered Nigel, glaring up at Frankie.

'You don't talk about Michael like that,' hissed Frankie.

'You did!'

'That's different.'

'How?'

'We're allowed,' explained Frankie. 'We're his friends. You're not.'

'Wouldn't want to be,' growled Nigel, clambering back up the slope.

'Wouldn't want you,' retorted Frankie.

'You lot are weirdos. Everybody knows that.'

'What?' snapped David.

'Not you,' said Nigel, hastily. 'Those two down there. And her. She's really weird.'

David took a step forward, ready to defend Frankie even though privately he thought Nigel had a point, but Frankie was already handling it.

'Why, thank you,' she said, smiling sweetly. Nigel opened his mouth to say something else but Frankie had already turned her back.

Nigel glowered but Frankie had instantly forgotten him. All her attention was focused once again on what was happening to Michael.

*

19

Miss Broadbent was crouching in front of him now. Her left eye was beginning to close as the flesh around it swelled up. Alice stared at the darkening skin, mesmerised. She could hardly believe that timid little Michael had just given a teacher a black eye.

'Michael?' said Miss Broadbent. 'Why don't you stop digging now?'

Michael ignored her. Warily, she reached forward and grasped his shoulder.

'Come on, sweetie. You can stop digging. It'll be all right.'

'No,' whimpered Michael, scrabbling frantically. 'There's no air down there.'

Miss Broadbent stood up and pulled a mobile phone from her shoulder bag.

'Alice, will you stay with him? I'm not going far. Just to the top of the dune to get a signal on this.' She waved the mobile phone. 'I'm going to call for some help. All right?'

Alice nodded.

'Good girl.' Miss Broadbent smiled and hurried off, thumbing buttons on her mobile phone. Alice was left alone with Michael. Moving slowly and quietly, she eased herself down onto the sand beside him. The hole was quite deep now. The sand was closely packed and the digging was harder. He was gasping for breath and his face was wet with sweat but he showed no sign of stopping.

'Michael,' she said in a small voice. 'You're really scaring me now.'

Michael kept on digging, hand over hand, and she stared at him, her eyes filling with tears. Miss

Broadbent was clambering up the slope behind her, and her classmates ringed the top of the dune but still she felt very alone.

Suddenly Michael let out a hiss and jerked his hands out of the hole. Alice blinked her tears away and saw that he was cradling one hand against his chest. She looked into his eyes and gave a small sob of relief because Michael was looking back at her. He was white-faced and bewildered but he was Michael again.

'I cut myself,' he said, simply, holding out his hand. The palm was filling up with blood. Alice shuffled forward on her knees and saw the bright gleam of broken glass in the bottom of the hole.

'Let me see,' she said, reaching for Michael's hand just as a trickle of blood overflowed his palm. Three drops the size of ten pence pieces landed in the hole and disappeared instantly, sucked into the sand. There was an instant of stillness that was somehow full of energy, like the instant before a wave curls over and crashes into the surf. Alice clutched Michael's injured hand in both of hers and hung on tight.

'What's going on?' she whispered.

Michael shook his head. '—I – I think we woke something up . . .'

Then the energy wave broke. There was nothing to see and nothing to hear but Alice felt something very powerful roll over her. Giddily, she slumped sideways and lay with her cheek against the sand. Up close she could see that each grain was vibrating minutely, moving so fast that the sand blurred in front of her eyes. It was as though a huge drum skin buried under the surface had just been struck.

The energy wave spread outwards and upwards, touching them all. Halfway up the slope, Miss Broadbent turned and took two uncertain steps back towards Alice and Michael. At the top of the dune, David moved closer to Frankie, protectively, and Nigel edged backwards away from the rim. Then it was over, gone before they had really begun to feel it.

Alice sat up, brushing the sand from her cheek. 'That was really weird,' she began, then froze into a frightened stillness. At the sound of her voice, Michael had gone into a fighting crouch, turning on her with the speed of a cornered animal. He looked at her without recognition, assessing her with eyes as hard and flat as silver coins. Alice began to tremble. She had known Michael for a long time, ever since they started school together. In all that time, she had never once been the slightest bit afraid of him, but now she was terrified. She slumped with relief when he dismissed her and turned his gaze to the top of the dune. He stiffened when he saw the others, then bent down without taking his eyes off them and pulled the shard of glass from the hole.

Alice looked up too and saw what he was seeing – a circle of black silhouettes standing still and silent with the sun glare behind them. A movement on the slope caught her eye. Miss Broadbent was hurrying back to them with a relieved smile on her face.

'You had me a bit worried there, Michael,' called the teacher. 'Are you feeling better?'

With a sort of dull horror, Alice saw Michael ease the hand holding the shard of glass behind his back.

She wanted to call out and warn Miss Broadbent but she knew without a shadow of a doubt that the glass would be used on her if she made a sound.

Miss Broadbent floundered on until she was close enough to see Michael's eyes, then her relieved smile faltered and she stumbled to a halt. Michael brought his hand out from behind his back and began to stride towards her, holding the glass shard like a dagger. He was two strides away from the bewildered teacher when a strangled electronic beeping brought him to a sudden halt. His hands fell to his sides and the tension left his shoulders. Even without seeing his face, Alice knew all the danger had drained out of him. Miss Broadbent tore her gaze away from Michael and stared stupidly down at the mobile phone in her hand for a few seconds before pressing a button and cutting it off in mid-beep.

'Oh, dear,' said Miss Broadbent, sounding nothing more than slightly irritated. 'I never finished dialling and now I've lost the signal. Still, you look much better, Michael. Are you all right?'

Michael held out the glass dagger and his injured hand. 'I cut myself.'

Alice scrambled to her feet and hurried over to Michael as fast as her trembling legs would allow. Miss Broadbent was busy inspecting Michael's cut, and the back of her neck as she bent over his hand looked very soft and vulnerable. Alice gripped Michael's other wrist, the one still holding the glass, and held it tight. She looked into his face and saw that his eyes were back to their usual gentle grey.

'I'll get rid of this, shall I?' she said, and he made

no objection when she eased the glass out of his hand. She turned her attention to Miss Broadbent.

'Are you all right, Miss?'

'Oh, yes. A bit of blood doesn't bother me.'

'No, I mean—'

'—this cut isn't too bad, really,' continued the teacher in a louder voice.

'—I mean, weren't you scared? Didn't you see—'

'—I don't think it needs stitches, just a clean up and a butterfly plaster.'

Alice stared at Miss Broadbent. Was it her imagination or was the teacher deliberately trying to drown her out? She had one more try at getting through.

'Miss, I'm not sure what just happened here, but—'

'Well then, let's ask Michael, shall we?' Miss Broadbent finally raised her head and looked into Michael's face. 'What do you think happened here, Michael?'

'I – I fell asleep. Then I had a really, really bad dream. But I fell asleep over there. And now I'm over here . . .' Michael's breath caught in his throat with a frightened little hitch. He stared down at the cut on his palm and his hand began to tremble. Then his face cleared and he looked up at Miss Broadbent with a relieved smile.

'I know what happened! I used to get them all the time but I haven't had one for years . . . They're called night terrors. It's when you have a nightmare and you wake up and start moving around and stuff, but you think you're still in the nightmare. I must've had a night terror – well, a day terror. Serves me right for falling asleep in the sun.'

24

'But—' Alice tugged at Michael's wrist. 'Come on! It was more than that. You weren't breathing. You were all blue . . .'

Michael slid Alice a sideways look and, just for an instant, she thought she saw the flat, silvery sheen in his eyes again. She blinked and let go of his wrist. When she looked again, he shrugged and gave her an embarrassed smile. 'Yeah, well, that's what my nightmare was about – not being able to breathe. I must've got too hot, sleeping in the sun. I dreamed I was down there, under the sand, in a sort of stone box—'

'Aha! So that's why you were digging!' exclaimed Miss Broadbent. 'You thought you were still buried!'

'Something like that,' said Michael.

Alice shook her head vigorously. 'No, hang on. Hang on. Michael, you'd stopped breathing. I had to thump you in the back—'

Michael looked down at his feet. 'I was probably holding my breath,' he muttered. 'I used to do that quite a lot, too.'

'But—'

'I think that's enough for now,' said Miss Broadbent, firmly, watching the rest of the group make their way down the slope of the dune with David and Frankie in the lead. 'You had a bit of a fright, Alice, so I can understand your need to dramatise things, but, really, you can see Michael is fine. Just look at him!'

'Do we have to?' said Frankie, walking up to Michael and giving him a swift but thorough inspection. Once she was sure he was more or less in one piece, she turned to stare at Miss Broadbent's rapidly blackening eye with open fascination. 'What's up?'

'Nothing's "up" as you put it,' said Miss Broadbent. 'Michael had a bit of a turn, that's all. Sunstroke, probably—'

'Cool! Was he hallucinating? Is that why he gave you that black eye?'

'Frankie! That's enough!'

'Oh, Miss,' said Michael in a trembling voice. 'I didn't, did I?'

'It was an accident,' interrupted Miss Broadbent, 'And I don't want to hear any more about it. Now, shall you and I stroll up to the mini-bus and crack open the first aid kit?'

'O.K.'

'And then I think we should all head back to the school. I know it's a bit early but I don't think we should stay here any longer.'

Alice had given up trying to persuade the teacher that something more than sunstroke had taken place in the dune hollow. Now she raised her head and looked at Miss Broadbent with new hope shining in her eyes. 'Why do you want to leave, Miss?'

'Well, I don't know whether anyone else felt that strange sort of – shift in the air a few minutes ago?'

Everyone nodded, especially Alice. David frowned. He could not deny he had felt something but he had no rational explanation for it, and that worried him.

'I think it was a change in the air pressure,' said Miss Broadbent.

'That would explain it, Miss,' said David with a

relieved smile, but Alice frowned and shook her head.

'I know what you're thinking, Alice,' said Miss Broadbent. 'I've never known the air pressure to change quite as dramatically as that either, but what else could it be?'

Alice opened her mouth then shut it again. She had no better answer.

'So. I think that means there's a storm on the way and—' Miss Broadbent pointed down at her thin summer dress. 'We're not exactly in the right gear for a storm.'

Everyone looked down at their own clothes. Alice automatically began to smooth the creases out of her new school skirt but then quickly pulled her hands back.

'Oops,' she said, staring down at herself. The light grey material was covered in dark red stains. For a moment she could not imagine what had happened, then she remembered kneeling in the sand and clutching Michael's bleeding hand in both of hers.

'Look.' She held out the front of her skirt for Frankie to see. 'Michael bled all over me.'

'Oh, my,' breathed Frankie. 'Your mom's going to—'

'Kill me,' finished Alice, flatly.

3

'Nail brush,' ordered Frankie, sticking one hand out behind her.

'Nail brush,' repeated Alice, slapping the brush into Frankie's outstretched palm.

Frankie leaned forward into the bath and scrubbed so hard her arm turned into a blur.

'Soap,' she panted, sticking out her other hand.

'Soap,' said Alice, handing over the bar from the washbasin. Frankie closed her fingers round the soap and returned to some serious scrubbing.

'Is it working?' asked Alice.

Frankie peered down into the bath. 'Don't know yet. There's too much foam. One more minute . . .'

Alice lowered the lid on the toilet seat and sat down, crossing her fingers. She and Frankie were locked in the tiny upstairs bathroom at her house. They had been trying to get the stains out of her school skirt for the past twenty minutes and Alice was expecting her mum to come knocking any time now. Footsteps pounded up the stairs and she glanced anxiously at the bathroom door, but the footsteps thudded past and into the boys' bedroom. Alice folded her long legs and brought her feet up onto the toilet seat, tucking her knees under her chin. The position made her think of Michael's still body, curled into a tight ball at the bottom of the dune. She frowned. What had happened at the beach earlier that afternoon? For a few, long minutes back there she had been convinced that Michael had turned into someone else, someone dangerous. Now, five hours later, the whole idea seemed ridiculous. She tried it out in her head – *I thought Michael was going to kill Miss Broadbent* – and giggled.

Frankie dropped the nail brush into the bath and sat back on her heels. 'What?' she grinned, ready to share the joke.

'I was just thinking about Michael . . .'

'Yeah! Trust him to give a teacher a black eye and get away with it!' Frankie ran fresh water into the bath and started to rinse out Alice's skirt.

'Yeah . . . Trust him. Um, Frankie? Did you think there was anything weird about this afternoon?'

'What, you mean apart from Michael?'

'Seriously.'

'O.K. Seriously, I did notice something kinda weird.' Frankie stopped rinsing and inspected the skirt. 'Hmmm, still yucky. Pass that bleach,' she ordered, sticking her hand out.

Alice did as she was told without thinking. 'What?' she asked. 'What did you notice?'

'Well . . .' Frankie carefully measured out a capful of bleach and dribbled it onto the bloodstains. 'Everyone was real grouchy. Me, you, David, creepy Nigel – a whole bunch of people – all of us nastier than a nest of hornets.'

'How was that weird?'

'Think about it. Last day of term – no lessons –

bright, sunshiney day. What's to be grouchy about? But I felt – I don't know – scratchy.'

'Scratchy?'

'Yeah. Scratchy. Like some of that sand had gotten under my skin, you know?'

Alice nodded, remembering her prickly bad temper with everyone and everything. 'I felt just the same. I wonder why?'

'Hey, weren't you paying attention? Our dear form tutor explained it all.'

'She did?'

'The pressure change, remember? Some people get a bit grouchy just before a storm. Nose bleeds and headaches and stuff like that.'

'Hmm. I suppose so. Funny, though.'

'What?'

'Well, the storm never arrived, did it?' Alice jumped as footsteps thundered past the door again, heading downstairs this time. 'Speaking of headaches,' she muttered.

'Which one was that, Kevin or Gary?'

'I don't know. They both crash around the house like baby elephants.'

'They're cute. It must be cool, having twin brothers.'

'You can come to their eighth birthday party if you want. All day Sunday on the beach. Sandy birthday cake and pass the parcel.' Alice scowled, struck once again by the unfairness of it all.

'I think I'll pass,' grinned Frankie. 'They're not that cute.'

'So,' said Alice, peering into the bath. 'Has it worked?'

'What?'

'The bleach.'

Frankie's eyes grew wide. She lunged for the skirt, turned the water on full and bent over the bath, rinsing frantically. After a few minutes she sat back on her heels and looked at Alice. 'O.K. The good news is, we got rid of the bloodstains.'

'And the bad news?'

'We got rid of the grey too.' Frankie held up the skirt. A large white patch looking rather like a map of South America was bleached into the front of it.

'Frankie!' shrieked Alice.

'I'm sorry! It always works when my mom does it!' Frankie flung the skirt into the bath. 'I think I left it on too long.'

Alice sighed. 'My mum's going to—'

'—kill you,' finished Frankie. 'I know. Oh! I know!' She sat up straight as an idea hit her. 'You can have my school skirt.'

'You can't give me your skirt.'

'Don't see why not, kiddo. I won't be needing it.' Frankie's smile slipped slightly. 'I'll be gone before the new school year starts.'

'Is it absolutely certain? I thought the oil company was offering your dad a new contract?'

'Yeah, but it looks like he's going to turn them down. He finishes work in three weeks' time. Mom's got some leave owing from the hospital. She's heading over here tonight on the red-eye flight to help us pack up.' Frankie sighed. 'You'd think a geophysicist and a surgeon would both be able to find work somewhere in the same continent, wouldn't you?'

31

They were both silent for a moment, thinking of the way adults could ruin everything without even trying.

'Parents,' said Alice, with feeling.

'Yeah.'

A knock on the door made them both jump.

'*Quick!*' hissed Alice, grabbing a bath towel and spreading it out on the floor. '*Skirt!*'

Frankie dropped the sopping skirt into the towel and Alice rolled it up in one neat movement. The doorknob turned once, then again.

'Alice . . .?'

'Coming, Mum. *Bleach* . . .!'

Alice shoved the bath towel into the back of the airing cupboard then hovered by the door with her hand on the bolt while Frankie fumbled to get the top back onto the bottle of bleach.

'Alice, are you all right . . .?'

'Yes. Hang on a minute—'

Frankie got the top on at the third attempt and flung the bottle under the sink. Alice pulled the bolt back just as the door handle began to rattle. The door swung open and they stood side by side, smiling brightly.

'What's going on?' said Mrs Mitchell.

'Um . . .' Alice looked at Frankie. Her head was completely empty.

'I . . .' Frankie glanced back at Alice and suddenly knew what to say. 'I was just about to cut Alice's hair for her.'

'Hmmm. Sounds like I knocked in the nick of time,' smiled Mrs Mitchell.

32

'What do you want?' asked Alice, remembering not to smile back.

'The gang's all here!'

'Pardon?' said Alice, stonily.

Mrs Mitchell sighed. 'Oh, that's right. I forgot. I'm getting the deep freeze treatment. David and Michael are here. They're at the back door.'

Somewhere between the top and the bottom of the stairs, Alice decided to put the afternoon behind her. Everything could be explained logically. Miss Broadbent was probably right, her fear at finding Michael in such a state had made her dramatise the incident with the shard of glass. Michael could no more kill someone than fly to the moon – and he had been absolutely fine on the way back from the beach. If Michael was happy to forget the afternoon, then so was she. Alice danced down the last few steps, light-headed with relief.

'What about the make-over?' complained Frankie, hurrying down the stairs after Alice.

'Some other time, I promise,' said Alice. 'Let's all go out together tonight. Celebrate the start of the summer holidays.'

'Sounds promising,' grinned Frankie as they reached the kitchen. 'What'll we do?'

'We could go down to the courts and play some tennis. Then get a pizza—'

'And a video and we could go back to my—' Frankie walked straight into Alice who had stopped dead in the middle of the kitchen. She stumbled backwards, rubbing her nose. 'Owww! Gimme some warning before you put on the brakes! Your back is so bony it's like walking into a – into a—' Frankie

33

gave up on trying to find a simile. '—a big, bony thing.'

Alice did not respond. She was staring at the open back door. Frankie side-stepped and peered over her shoulder. David and Michael were standing side by side, waiting for them. Michael was cradling his bandaged hand and David had a shovel slung over one shoulder.

'What's happening?' asked Frankie.

Michael looked over at David, waiting for him to speak.

'He wants to go back,' said David.

Michael was aware of an uneasy silence as they walked away from Alice's house. Frankie was chattering away as usual, but she could talk for hours without needing a reply, so that didn't really count. Underneath the chatter there was a silence and the silence was coming from Alice and David. Michael stumbled along between them, glancing unhappily from one to the other.

David was marching along, swinging the shovel and refusing to return Michael's pleading looks. Michael swallowed miserably. He knew why David was angry. David thought a return trip to the beach was a complete waste of time, but Michael had insisted on it. He had to go back and finish digging that hole. The nightmare had been so real, he had to prove to himself that there was nothing down there.

As for Alice, Michael was not sure why she was so quiet, but he had a good idea. He could remember being in the nightmare and he could remember standing in front of Miss Broadbent, showing her his cut hand, but the time in between was just a fuzzy blur. Of course, at the first opportunity, Frankie had told him all about it. She had sat in the mini-bus while Miss Broadbent cleaned and bandaged his hand, telling him how gross the cut looked and describing his frantic hole-digging in gleeful detail. Alice had stayed outside, looking pale and shocked. Michael thought that probably his behaviour had not been so funny close-up. He guessed that he must have scared Alice pretty badly.

Now he glanced over and saw that she was watching him out of the corner of her eye. Alice smiled and quickly looked away, but not before he saw the puzzled, wary look on her face. It hurt him to see that look. She had been his friend and protector ever since they started school together and now she was looking at him as though she did not know who he was. Michael reached out and touched her arm.

'Thanks for looking after me on the beach,' he said.

Alice nodded.

Michael tried again. 'I'm sorry if I scared you—'

'If it was only a night terror,' interrupted Alice, 'then why do you want to go back now? Can't you just forget about it?'

'I spent the last five hours trying to do just that, but—' Michael shook his head, remembering how he had wandered around the flat, leaving a trail of half-eaten sandwiches, half-watched videos and half-read books. '—I couldn't get the nightmare out of my head. It was like an itch, right in the middle of my brain, and the itch got worse and worse until I decided the only way to scratch it was to go back to the beach. So, I phoned David – and here we are.'

Alice said nothing. They walked on a few more paces in silence and Michael winced as he realised that Alice was gradually edging away from him towards the other side of the pavement.

'Look, whatever happened down at the beach, you know it was only me,' he said.

Alice turned and stared at him with startled, hopeful eyes. Without understanding why, Michael saw that he had just blurted out exactly what she wanted to hear.

'It was only me,' he said again, and held his breath. Alice hesitated, then the wary look left her face.

'I know,' she said and finally gave him a proper smile. Michael grinned back, full of relief.

'Well, you might be talking to him again,' grumbled David. 'But I'm not. He phones me up, saying he has to go back to the beach. Now. Tonight. Won't take no for an answer.'

David scowled at Michael and was annoyed to see that Michael was smiling back at him, happily.

'Never mind that we're just building up to the harvest on the farm. Never mind that my dad wants me to help him get the combine ready. Oh, no. I have to get on my bike and pedal all the way into town with a shovel strapped to my back—'

David looked at Michael again and saw that his smile was even wider. 'Well, aren't you going to say anything?'

'Um . . . Thank you?' said Michael.

'Oh, forget it. Let's go and dig this hole and get it over with.'

'Can we come?' piped a voice behind them.

Alice stopped dead and, once again, Frankie cannoned into her back.

'Owww! Gimme a break!'

Alice ignored her. She was too busy glaring at Kevin and Gary, who were standing side by side on the pavement with identical hopeful smiles on their faces.

'Uh, oh,' said Frankie, standing back to let Alice deal with them.

'Go home,' ordered Alice.

'But we're good at digging holes,' said Kevin.

'I said go home!'

Gary pouted. 'But we want to go to the beach,' he whined.

'Well I'm not taking you.'

Gary and Kevin looked at one another and, as though at some pre-arranged signal, their eyes began to fill up with tears.

'Until Sunday,' amended Alice, hastily. 'We're all going to the beach on Sunday, for your party, remember?'

The twins looked at one another again, then nodded.

'Right then, see you,' said Alice. The twins did not move. 'Come on,' she said to the other three. 'Just leave them.'

They all set off again. The twins trailed along behind, but at a slower pace. 'They'll give up soon,' said Alice. 'Ignore them.'

'What about him?' said Frankie, jerking her chin down the road ahead. 'Do we ignore him, too?'

Nigel Dunn was walking towards them with a

football tucked into the crook of his arm. David groaned and attempted to hide the shovel behind his back. As they drew closer, Nigel glanced at Michael, Frankie and Alice, then dismissed them as usual and focused on David.

'Hey, David,' he called. 'Fancy a kick-about? We're all meeting up at the park.'

Frankie winked at Alice then moved up in front of Nigel, dancing on her toes, dodging and weaving. 'I'll play!' she sang. 'I'm good at soccer.'

'No.'

'Go on! On me 'ead, son!' called Frankie, in a very bad cockney accent.

'Get lost.'

Frankie lunged forward and attempted to knock the ball out of the crook of his arm but Nigel was too fast for her. 'No girls allowed!' he yelled.

Frankie shrugged and sauntered off behind his back.

'So,' said Nigel, giving Frankie a wary glance over his shoulder before turning to David. 'You coming?'

Michael suddenly became very interested in a piece of dried mud on the toe of his trainer. He knew what David's answer was going to be and he did not want to see Nigel's face when it came.

'No thanks,' said David.

Michael grimaced as he knocked the mud from his trainer and crushed it under his foot. The thing was, even though Nigel treated him like that piece of mud, Michael felt sorry for him. Nigel could never quite believe that David did not want to be his friend. They were made to be best friends; everyone could see that. They were both popular at school and

38

good at sport. They even looked alike. Nigel was a watered-down version of David with thinner hair and paler eyes, but still, they could have been brothers.

And we would have been friends, thought Michael. *If Nigel didn't have a sly streak a mile wide.* Michael looked up and saw that Nigel's face had gone a dull red. He bit his lip and waited for things to get nasty.

'No thanks,' mimicked Nigel. 'You know, David, we're all starting to wonder about you.'

'Really?' said David.

'We're wondering why you hang around with two weird girls and the looney digger over there.'

'Because otherwise I'd have to hang around with you.'

Nigel looked David up and down and finally caught sight of the shovel. His pale eyes glinted. 'What's the shovel for?'

'Bait digging,' said David, promptly. 'We're going fishing tomorrow.'

'Where're you going to put the bait – in your pockets?'

'What?'

'You haven't got a bait bucket, you prat! So, what are you up to?'

Suddenly, the football blasted out of the crook of Nigel's arm and shot off down the street. He turned to see Frankie standing right behind him, rubbing her knuckles.

'I'm good at volleyball, too,' she said, smugly. 'Go on, then! Run after your ball!'

For a second it looked as though Nigel was going to hit Frankie but then he got himself under control and pounded off down the street after his ball. David grinned at Frankie and suddenly realised how much he was going to miss her. He blinked with surprise. Frankie was one of the most irritating people he knew. She was loud, opinionated, bossy and unpredictable and, when she first muscled in on their group nearly a year ago, he had hated her. Now he realised he did not want her to go back to America. She had become a part of the group.

'Well don't just stand there!' ordered Frankie. 'Let's get outa here.'

As he hurried after Frankie, Michael could feel the skin between his shoulder blades prickling and realised he was half expecting Nigel's ball or Nigel's fist to slam into the back of his head. He risked one nervous glance over his shoulder and frowned. Nigel was not creeping up on them. He was deep in conversation with the twins. As Michael slowed down, trying to figure out how much the twins had heard about the return trip to the beach, Nigel raised his head and stared down the road straight at him. Michael stumbled and quickly turned away. The others had already disappeared round the corner at the bottom of Alice's street and he ran to catch up. Just before he turned onto Border Road, Michael glanced back once more and wished he hadn't. Nigel was standing with his arms folded, waiting for him to look. As soon as he turned round, Nigel made his hand into a gun, pointed it straight at Michael and pretended to pull the trigger.

4

'What the heck is that?' asked Frankie, coming to a sudden stop. They had reached the headland, which was the highest point on the road between the town and the beach. From there, it was possible to see both the town and harbour to the North and the beach to the South. Except the beach had vanished.

'I said, what the heck is that?' repeated Frankie as the others came panting up behind her. She pointed down to the place where the beach should have been. Up on the headland, the late evening sun was still warming their faces and the sky was a cloudless blue. Below them, the beach was hidden by a shifting bank of fog. It was like looking down into a basin of dry ice.

'That's a haar,' said David.

'Come again?'

'A haar. A sea fret. Speciality of the East coast. But this can't be the first time you've seen one?'

'It probably is, you know,' said Alice. 'Frankie and her dad arrived here last September. Summer was over by then and you only get haars in the summer.'

'So you're telling me this is, like, a special summery fog?' asked Frankie. 'Gimme a break!'

David folded his arms and settled down to explaining a haar. 'Sometimes on this coast, when the tide turns and comes back in, it brings a haar with it. It happens when the weather's been very hot, like today, and it's something to do with warm air meeting cold sea water. I think.'

'That's just typical of this crazy place,' grumbled Frankie. 'We get three weeks in the whole year when the sun shines, and this – this har-de-har thingummy comes along and puts the beach out of action!'

'It's not just the beach, Frankie,' said Alice. 'Look behind you.'

Frankie turned and blinked. The whole of the coastline, including the town and the harbour, had a cotton wool edging of fog. 'How did that get there?'

'It comes in fast, once it gets going,' said David. 'See?' He pointed down the road, where smoky ten-drils of fog were curling up towards them. 'Now that's going to spread a few miles inland, then it'll stop, just like that, as though there's an invisible line it won't cross.'

'Well, whoopie-doo,' muttered Frankie. 'Good for the haar. All I know is it aint gonna be as much fun as I thought down on that beach tonight.'

'Yeah,' said Michael, speaking for the first time since they reached the headland. 'Maybe this wasn't such a good idea.' His voice wavered slightly and Alice glanced at him anxiously. He was staring down into the fog and his eyes looked huge in his pale face. Alice felt the hairs on the back of her neck rise up in a shivering line.

'We could always go and get that pizza,' she began, but David was already marching up to Michael with a determined look on his face.

'No way,' he growled, planting one hand between

Michael's shoulder blades and propelling him down the road towards the beach. 'No way are you changing your mind now. We're going down there and we're going to dig that stupid hole.'

Alice looked at Frankie. 'I'm starting not to like this,' she said.

Frankie shrugged. 'Yeah, but nothing's going to stop Davey-boy in that mood. Besides, what can a bit of fog do to us? Dampen us to death? Come on. Let's just get it over with.'

Frankie headed off down the road after the boys but Alice hung back, twisting her long hair around her fingers. In the safety of her bathroom, she had convinced herself that she was being silly about the beach, but now, every nerve in her body was telling her not to go back there. For a few seconds more, she stood her ground as the other three moved further down the road, but the thought of watching them disappear into the fog without her was too much.

'Wait for me!' she called and sprinted down the road after them.

The fog did not swallow them all at once. At first there were only ragged scraps of it, drifting like smoke and raising gooseflesh on their bare arms. Above them the sun shone and, when they looked over their shoulders, they could still see the headland. Gradually, as they descended into the bay, the scraps of fog thickened into a solid, encircling wall, the sharp cries of the sea birds faded away and the sun became a dirty, yellow disc. Finally, the sun was blotted out and only a cold, milky light filtered through to them as they reached the bottom of the hill. They walked on and the fog opened out in front of them and closed in behind them, so that they always seemed to be at the centre of a small clearing.

'Have we reached the car park yet?' asked Alice, peering into the fog.

'Dunno,' said David. 'It's hard to judge distances in this stuff.'

'This is crazy,' moaned Frankie, shivering in her thin T-shirt. 'If we can't even find the car park, how are we going to find the right bit of sand to dig up?' She turned to Michael. 'I mean, it's not as though you planted a flag or anything.'

Michael hesitated. 'Maybe if we got onto the beach – I think I could find my way from there . . .'

'Let's go then,' said David decisively. 'Look, here's one of those little paths.'

'But – how do you know it's the right one?' asked Alice.

'Doesn't matter. They all lead to the beach.' David left the road and headed off along a sandy track which meandered away through the grass. Frankie followed at his heels, but Alice and Michael both hesitated. The road was their last link with the town on the other side of the headland and Michael felt a great reluctance to leave the smooth black tarmac.

'All right?' asked Alice, watching him carefully.

Michael lifted his head and gave her a slightly wobbly smile. 'Fine! I'm fine,' he said and stepped off the road.

'Gee, this is fun,' muttered Frankie a few minutes later, as they teetered across slippery piles of stones and seaweed left by the tide at the top of the beach. They kept their eyes down, choosing where to step, but still the odd stone shifted under their feet and bounced away into the fog, hitting against other stones with a dull, short clack, like colliding billiard balls. It was the only sound on the beach. Even the sea was quiet.

Once clear of the stones, they stopped concentrating on their feet and lifted their heads to look around them as they walked. What they saw was in stark contrast to the long, sunny stretch of beach they had walked along that afternoon. Six metres away in every direction, the fog swirled. The sea was grey and flat. Waves slid silently up the beach with an oily smoothness and the sand was no longer a dazzling, silky white but a dirty brown, with a wet crust on the surface.

Without realising they were doing it, they moved closer together. There was a wrongness about the place which they could all feel, but no one wanted to put it into words.

'Not exactly buzzing, is it?' said Frankie, lightly.

'Nobody here but us,' agreed Alice.

'And them,' said David, pointing. They all turned to look at a small group of eider ducks that had floated into view just offshore. The ducks stared steadily back at them with their beady black eyes. David frowned and clapped his hands, once, twice. The ducks did not even ruffle their smart black and white feathers. They drifted along on the current and continued to stare blankly until the fog swallowed them up again.

'They're used to people, that's all,' said David, a little too loudly.

Michael came to a sudden halt. 'I think we should head into the dunes now,' he said.

'How the heck do you know?' asked Frankie, waving her arms at the enclosing fog.

'I recognise that rock,' lied Michael, beginning to climb the dune slope. He could not explain how he knew the hollow was waiting for them on the other side of this particular dune, but it was there. He could feel it.

They reached the top of the dune and peered down the other side. Fog had poured into the hollow below like milk into a bowl.

'I can't see a thing,' said David.

Michael thought about what might be hiding under the fog layer and he shuddered.

'Yeah, I'm cold too,' said Frankie, rubbing at her bare arms.

'It's the fog,' said Alice.

'Yeah . . .'

For a few seconds they all stood poised on the lip of the hollow, each waiting for someone else to call the whole thing off, but no one spoke and the moment passed.

'Right,' said David. He took a firmer grip on his shovel and headed off down the slope. The others had started to follow when suddenly David gave a yell. His arms jerked up in the air and he disappeared below the fog layer as though something had dragged him in.

For a frozen moment, Alice, Michael and Frankie stared at one another, their eyes wide with shock. Frankie shook her head as though refusing to believe what she had just seen and hundreds of tiny droplets of condensation danced on her wiry black curls. Alice watched the shimmering droplets with a sort of panicked concentration.

'He's gone,' said Michael, stupidly.

Then David's head poked up through the blanket of fog and grinned at them. 'Well, I just found the hole,' he said.

David started by widening and squaring off the hole, then he got down to the business of digging. He handled the shovel well, slicing it crisply into the wet sand then putting his weight behind the lift. By the time he clambered out for a rest, the hole was nearly half a metre deep.

After that they all took turns. It was satisfying work and they settled into a steady rhythm. The fog cocooned them in a white silence, punctuated by the regular crunch of the shovel, and Michael became so involved in the task, he quite forgot why they were doing it.

'Happy?' said David, finally, leaning on the shovel and gazing up at him.

Michael blinked with surprise. 'What?'

David moved up to the edge of the hole and threw the shovel onto the floor of the hollow. 'It's waist deep now,' he said patiently. 'And it's getting too packed and stony to dig much further. There's nothing here, Michael. Or if there is, it's too deep for us to reach.'

'O.K.' said Frankie, suddenly bored. 'Let's go eat. I'm starving.'

'Hang on a minute,' said David. 'We can't leave it like this. We have to fill it in again.'

'Whaaaat!' shrieked Frankie. 'You can't be serious!' Her high voice pierced through the fog and a shower of sand trickled from the dune slope above the hole, pattering down onto David's head.

'See,' he said, turning to inspect the slope. 'We've undermined it a bit. We have to fill the hole in again. It could be dange—'

David never managed to finish what he was saying. Suddenly, a huge, clotted lump of dune broke away and slid into the hole with a heavy sigh, burying him completely. For an instant the three of them stared stupidly at the spot where David had been, then Michael and Alice both fell onto their knees and started digging furiously.

Frankie grabbed the shovel and was about to drive it into the sand when Alice spotted her.

'No!' shouted Alice. 'You might hit him!'

Frankie dropped the shovel and threw herself down beside Alice just as David's hand came clawing out of the sand. She grabbed it and hung on tight, while Alice and Michael dug down on either side of his arm.

'We've got you, Davey,' she whispered. 'Hang on, we've got you.'

'Here!' yelled Michael, brushing the sand away from the top of David's head. 'I've found him.'

Alice scooped out handfuls of wet sand and uncovered David's face. His eyes and mouth were squeezed shut. She dragged her sleeve down over her hand and wiped his face clean.

'Oh, look!' she cried as his eyes opened. 'He's all right.'

David tilted his head back as far as it would go and

opened his mouth wide, searching for some air. His eyes bulged and he tried to say something, but no sound came out.

'What's the matter with him?' sobbed Frankie. 'Why can't he breathe?'

Suddenly, Michael understood what was wrong. 'Quick! He's all folded up under there – we've got to take the pressure off his rib cage.'

They dug as fast as they could, clearing sand away from his chest and back until David could sit up and pull air into his lungs without difficulty.

'You took your time,' he spluttered, as soon as he could talk. He blinked the sand away and squinted up at them. Three anxious faces stared back at him. 'It's all right,' he said, giving them a weak smile. 'I can hold my breath for ages.'

'Boasting again,' said Frankie, with a little hiccup of tears in her voice.

David frowned with concentration as he wriggled his hips back and forth in the sand. Then an expression of triumph crossed his face as he managed to lift one knee clear. He held his hands out to them. 'Grab hold,' he said. 'I think I'll be able to climb out now if you give me a lift.'

Michael and Alice grabbed an arm each and Frankie cleared more sand away until finally David pulled the other leg clear and clambered to his feet. He was caked with wet sand from head to foot and he had lost his trainers but otherwise he seemed to have survived his brief burial unharmed. Impulsively, Alice hugged him fiercely and he let her do it, grinning at Frankie and Michael over her shoulder.

'Here you are,' said Michael, retrieving David's trainers and holding them out to him.

'Give them to me,' tutted Alice, letting go of David and grabbing the trainers. 'They're full of sand! He can't wear them like that!'

Alice began bashing the trainers together briskly and David rolled his eyes at Michael. 'Especially when the rest of me is looking so smart,' he said.

Michael snorted with surprised laughter and stepped forward to help David scrape the wet sand from his clothes.

'Well,' said Frankie. 'At least we don't have to fill in the hole now.'

'Frankie!' gasped Michael.

'What? He's O.K. isn't he? You're O.K. aren't you, Davey? A bit damp and smelly, but, hey, what's new?'

Frankie grinned at David but he had stopped trying to clear the sand from his ears and was standing with his arms folded, frowning at her.

'Only kidding,' said Frankie, but David's frown deepened. Frankie sighed. She hated having to say sorry, but he seemed to be expecting it. She leaned forward to whisper a quick apology and realised that David had not been looking at her at all. He was staring at the dune slope behind her with a puzzled look on his face.

'What's that?' said David.

Michael felt icy fingers touch the back of his neck. He turned round and looked at the place where the dune had collapsed, already knowing what he was going to see. A little way up the slope, the broken remains of a curved stone wall were now protruding from the side of the dune and, wedged upright into what had once been a hidden recess in the wall, was a narrow, slab-sided stone box.

'Oh, my!' said Frankie. 'Would you look at that?'

'Michael?' said Alice, moving up beside him. 'How can that be? It's the stone box from your dream, isn't it?'

'No,' said Michael, shaking his head vigorously.

'But you said you were trapped in a stone.'

'No! It was only a dream! It can't be the same one.' Michael licked his lips and tasted salt. He bent over and tried to retch. Alice automatically laid a cool hand on the back of his neck the way her mother did when she was sick, but she continued to stare at the stone box with wide eyes.

Frankie and David climbed up the slope to take a closer look. 'It looks really – old,' said Frankie.

'That's your expert opinion, is it?' asked David.

'Shut up,' said Frankie, mildly, leaning closer to the box. 'D'you think there might be some treasure in it?'

David shrugged. 'I know what Michael thinks.'

'What?'

'He thinks there's a body in it.'

'Nah,' said Frankie. 'No way. It's too small for that.'

David reached out and touched the rough hewn stone of the box, then quickly jerked his hand away.

'What's the matter?' said Frankie.

'Cold,' said David, briefly. 'And a bit . . . slimey.'

'Yeah, well it would be, wouldn't it?' said Frankie. 'It's been buried under the dune just about for ever. Let's open it up.' Casually, she picked up the shovel and wedged it behind the front slab of the box before any of them realised what she was doing.

'Wait!' yelled Michael, lunging forward, but Frankie had already put all her weight against the shovel handle, using it like a lever. With a loud crack, the stone slab broke neatly in two. There was a sound something like a sigh and they all took a step back as they caught the musty smell of stale air. The bottom piece of the slab stayed where it was, wedged into the wall, but the top piece began to tilt slowly outwards.

'Get back!' called David. 'It's going to fall!'

They backed away from the slope and waited. First the shovel slipped out of the widening gap and somersaulted down into the hollow, clanging against the wall as it went, then the broken piece of slab fell away from the box and embedded itself in the sand at their feet with a dull thud.

For a few seconds they stood, statue-still, gazing up at the black opening in the front of the stone box. Even Frankie seemed taken aback by what she had just done.

'I – didn't think it would break like that,' she said hesitantly. 'I didn't think it would be so easy . . .'

'Well, you've done it now,' said David, grimly.

'Don't sound so shocked,' she said. 'You wanted it open. Didn't you?'

'No,' said Michael, gazing fearfully at the box. 'I don't think I did.'

'O.K. Apart from Michael. Alice – David – you're not telling me you would have walked away without opening it?'

'You should have let us talk about it first,' said David.

'Why?' said Frankie, beginning to sound annoyed. 'You would've decided to open it anyway, I know you would. I just saved you ten minutes of boring, boring talk, that's all.'

Alice nodded, grudgingly. 'She's right. We have to look.'

Michael took a deep breath and armed the sweat from his face. 'So,' he said. 'Let's look.'

He stepped up to the bottom of the slope. Alice, David and Frankie joined him and, together, they climbed towards the box.

5

They drew level with the stone box and peered inside. There was an instant of stunned silence, then Frankie turned and ran back down the slope. Alice gasped and clapped both hands over her mouth and David shook his head slowly from side to side as though he could not accept what he was seeing. Michael was the only one who did not react with shock. He felt nothing but a tired recognition as he gazed at the small, dried-up body squatting inside the box.

'Oh, the poor thing,' said Alice, her voice trembling with sadness. 'It's a little girl, isn't it?'

David grimaced as he took a second look at the shrivelled figure. He could tell it was a child because of the size, but that was all. The body was nothing more than a skeleton held together by a tissue-thin layer of yellow skin which looked as dry and fragile as old paper. The torso was draped in the remnants of a woollen garment which still carried a faint checked pattern in the weave.

'I can't tell,' he said.

'But look at her hair. See that long plait?'

David felt his stomach roll greasily, but he swallowed hard and peered into the stone box again. Only wispy strands of hair remained clinging to the

54

skull but the plait at the nape of the neck had survived intact. It was long and fair, and it was smeared with some sort of thick paste, which made the end stick out stiffly like a paint brush.

'Yeah, I see it,' said David.

'Oh, Michael,' whispered Alice. 'Look at her sweet little face.'

Michael's face was bleak as he stared into the stone box. The child was squatting with her hands clasped around her ankles and her head resting on her knees, just as he had been in his nightmare. Her face was turned towards the opening as though she was trying to look out at them, but her eyelids drooped tiredly over empty eye sockets. She still had long, fair eyelashes which curved down to rest on her sharp cheekbones. Only the bridge of her nose was left, curving like a beak over elongated nostrils. The lips were gone too, and the gums had shrivelled away, exposing long, yellow teeth which made Michael think of the mouth of a horse. He lifted his gaze from her mouth to her forehead and moaned deep in his throat when he saw how the skin had split along the frown lines.

'There's some stuff in the bottom of the box,' said David, leaning forward for a closer look. 'Rough crystals of some sort.'

'Salt,' said Michael, briefly, without even looking.

'Yes, I think you're right,' said David, sending Michael a surprised glance.

'I wonder how she died?' asked Alice.

'She didn't,' said Michael, taking in the shredded skin on the child's elbows. He switched his gaze to the hands and winced when he saw that the finger ends were torn and blackened. 'What I mean is, she wasn't dead when they put her in there.'

'That's a horrible thing to say!' said Alice, beginning to cry.

'And it's not true,' added David.

A stubborn look came over Michael's face. 'I'm telling you, she was alive when they put her in there—'

'Shut up! You're upsetting Alice! This is obviously a really old stone tomb – it's hundreds, maybe thousands of years old. I think she must have died of some childhood illness they couldn't cure, and when she died, they mummified her. That's what the salt's for. Salt's a preservative, isn't it?'

Michael clenched his fists and glared at David. All of a sudden he could not understand why they had ever been friends. 'You always think you're so right! Well you're not right this time! She was alive—'

'Shut up,' growled David, glancing at Alice just as another tear rolled down her cheek. He raised his fists as a great desire to punch Michael came over him. The two boys squared up to one another.

'Stop it!' ordered Alice, trying to edge between them.

'Guys?' called Frankie, from the bottom of the slope. 'I want to go home.' Her voice sounded very young and very scared but all Alice heard was Frankie being her usual selfish self.

'I want?' yelled Alice, storming down the slope to Frankie. 'I want?' She pushed Frankie hard in the chest, knocking her to the ground. 'I'll tell you what you want. You want to start noticing there are other people in this world apart from you!'

Frankie cringed on the wet sand and Alice stood over her, breathing hard. There was a look in her eyes that Frankie had never seen before. It made Frankie want to run. 'I'm sorry, Alice,' she said. 'Don't hit me . . .'

Alice blinked. She had been filled with a furious anger but it all drained out of her in a split second. 'Hit you? I wouldn't hit you.' She frowned down at Frankie, then suddenly raised her head and looked around the foggy hollow as though trying to spot where such anger had come from. David and Michael were hurrying towards her, their own fight forgotten. They were both staring at her as though she had grown another head. Alice reached out her hand to help Frankie up and, after a slight hesitation, Frankie took it.

'Listen, there's something not right here,' said Alice, hauling Frankie to her feet. 'This afternoon, we were all edgy, remember? And now the same thing's happening again only worse. We should leave before something else happens.'

'I think it might be too late for that,' said David.

He pointed to the top of the hollow and they all stared up into the swirling fog. Alice grabbed for Frankie's hand and Michael felt his spine prickle with fear. Something was up there, a dark, hump-backed shape half-hidden in the fog.

'It's stalking us,' breathed Frankie and they each nodded in agreement. Even though they could see nothing but a vague, humped outline, there was a poised stillness about the shape which made them certain they were being watched. Instinctively, they moved backwards together until they were huddled in a tight bunch with the curved wall behind them.

'We could make a run for it,' whispered David. The creature in the fog gave a low, menacing growl and loomed closer.

'What is that thing?' whimpered Frankie.

'There's more than one,' said Michael. 'Look.'

Horrified, they watched as the shape split into three. The largest of the creatures stayed in place while the second one moved around the rim of the hollow to the left and the third peeled off to the right.

'It's as though they heard me,' said David in a low voice, as the shapes circled round to cut off any possible escape route.

'What now?' said Alice, trying to keep the trembling out of her voice,

David bent and picked up the shovel. 'Now they'll move in,' he said.

He was right. Alice felt her heart give a lurch as a second low growl came from the largest of the shapes and three figures began to materialise out of the fog. Part of her really did not want to find out what could make such a dreadful sound, but she kept watching. It would be worse not to know.

They emerged from the fog and stood on the rim of the dune for a few seconds, staring down into the hollow. Their thick fur was the colour of fog, their eyes blazed yellow and their tongues lolled from their mouths like pieces of bright red ribbon.

'They're—' Alice stopped. She had been going to say . . . But, no, that was impossible, wasn't it? Her brain rejected the idea and she shook her head, feeling a dreamy numbness steal over her. David, Michael and Frankie seemed to be feeling the same way because they were all staring up at the top of the dune as though they were watching a show.

The creatures began to move down the dune slope, stepping lightly on their long, thin legs and placing their paws with dainty precision, like graceful ballerinas. As they drew closer, Alice caught a strong, musky scent. Her nostrils flared at the hot, animal smell and her eyes widened as she came out of her trance.

'Wolf!' she shrieked. 'They're wolves!'

Frankie filled her lungs and let out a high, frightened scream. The wolves stopped in their tracks. All three of them laid their ears flat against their skulls and their muzzles puckered into soundless snarls. Frankie watched their black lips pulling back over long, yellow fangs and she screamed again. The smallest wolf flinched at the noise and glanced at the leader. David noticed the glance and a ghost of a plan flitted into his head.

'O.K. They don't like noise,' he said. 'Listen, everybody. I want you to wait till I start yelling, then join in as loudly as you can.'

David hefted the shovel in his hands and stepped in front of Michael, Frankie and Alice. He had decided to handle the wolves the same way as he and his dad handled the cattle on the farm. 'If you want to be the boss,' he muttered, 'you act like the boss.' He was shaking, but he made himself take another step towards the wolves. Then he planted his feet solidly in the sand and stood as tall as he could.

'Aaaahhhh!' he howled, brandishing the shovel

above his head like a weapon. Behind him the others joined in, yelling and screaming and clapping their hands together for all they were worth.

It very nearly worked. The noise sent the two smaller wolves cringing into the slope until their bellies scraped the sand, but the lead wolf stood firm. It took three stiff-legged steps towards David, then went down on its haunches and prepared to pounce.

David stared into the merciless yellow eyes and felt his mouth go dry. He stopped yelling and behind him the others stuttered raggedly to a halt. For another second he stood his ground, but his courage was draining away. He swallowed and his throat clicked loudly in the silence, then he dropped the shovel and took a faltering backwards step.

The wolf launched itself at David, and a green and yellow striped rubber ball bounced into the hollow between them.

'Fetch, Daisy!' called a voice from the top of the dune. The wolf twisted, caught the ball in mid-air and came down in the sand. Then it turned in a blur of teeth and fur and headed for David. He went into a half-crouch, covering his head with his arms, and waited for the pain to start. Nothing happened for a few seconds, then something cold and wet touched his leg just above the ankle.

'David,' said Alice in a voice soft with wonder. 'Look . . .'

Cautiously, he lowered his arms and looked down. The green and yellow ball was lying on the ground at his feet and a large, grey, shaggy mongrel was gazing up at him with a pleading expression in its dark brown eyes.

'What . . .?' David snapped his head up and stared wild-eyed around the hollow, looking for the other two wolves. They were nowhere in sight. Instead he saw a sturdy little Border Terrier dancing excitedly around Frankie's legs and a young Labrador, lying on its back, waiting for a white-faced Michael to stroke it.

'What's going on?' wailed Frankie.

David shook his head, lost for words.

'They – changed,' said Alice, in a dazed voice. 'I saw it. Well, not exactly saw it, but . . .' She stopped and ran her shaking hands through her hair, then tried again. 'They were wolves. And then the ball came. And then they were dogs. A . . . And there was just an instant, only one instant, when they were – between.'

'Between?' repeated David, stupidly, looking down at the mongrel sitting at his feet and waiting for him to throw the ball.

'They – the air sort of shimmered. And then I was looking at three dogs. And it seemed as though they had always been dogs.'

Michael nodded. 'Dogs,' he agreed, reaching down and prodding the Labrador's belly with a tentative finger.

A piercing whistle came from the top of the dune and the three dogs raced up the slope to meet their owner.

'Here we go again,' muttered David, picking up the shovel. They moved back into their tight group and waited in silence to see what else was going to come out of the fog. First a pair of sturdy boots appeared, then some very old combat pants,

61

followed by an ancient leather jacket topped with a head of long brown hair twisted into thick dread-locks and pulled back into a loose ponytail.

'Dog Boy!' yelped Frankie, her voice shrill with relief. 'It's Dog Boy!'

Alice let her breath out in a whoosh of air and Michael sat down very suddenly on the sand. David lowered the shovel and leaned on it as all the strength suddenly went out of his legs.

Dog Boy was a familiar figure in the town. He had arrived with the tourists three summers ago and had simply stayed on, earning enough from the odd casual job to keep himself and his dogs fed. Other-wise, he spent his time working as a volunteer at the swan sanctuary or taking part in beach clean-ups. Whenever there was an eco-protest, he was there, in the thick of it. When the council had proposed a seagull cull because of the mess the birds made, he had dumped a bucket of whitewash on the town hall steps as a protest. He walked his dogs twice a day, whatever the weather and, although he rarely spoke to other walkers, he always gave them a friendly smile.

He was not smiling now. His face was deadly serious as he loped across the floor of the hollow towards them.

'Um – your dogs—' Frankie stopped, wondering how to explain what had happened, but Dog Boy was not listening.

'Stay!' he ordered, and his three dogs immediately sank down onto the sand. Dog Boy walked straight past Frankie and up the opposite slope of the dune. He stopped in front of the stone box and stared inside for a long moment, then he stepped back and gazed around the hollow, looking for something.

'Your dogs—' began Frankie again.

'I know,' said Dog Boy, shortly. 'And I know why it happened. But first—' He broke off as he spotted the missing piece of stone slab lying in the sand. 'Just let me do this, O.K.?' Quickly, he lifted the slab and slotted it back into place, then he grabbed the shovel from David and set about reburying the stone box using the left over sand from the hole they had dug. He worked fast, flinging shovel loads of wet sand up the slope as though it was as light as popcorn, and in a very short time the pile and the box had both disappeared.

'Thanks,' he said, holding the shovel out to David. 'Now, we need to get out of here.'

'But we're still waiting for an explanation—' began David.

'Not here,' interrupted Dog Boy.

'But—'

Dog Boy moved up close and stared into David's face. Alice, standing next to David, noticed two startling things. First, Dog Boy's eyes were different colours. One was bright blue, the other was green. Second, he was as frightened as they were.

'We need to get out of here,' said Dog Boy, gazing at each of their dazed, frightened faces. 'Now.'

'Where are we going to go?' quavered Frankie, her eyes big with tears.

Dog Boy looked at the four of them, shivering in their thin summer clothes. 'Come on,' he decided. 'My place is just the other side of the headland. And you all look like you need a strong cup of tea.'

6

Dog Boy's place was an old caravan at the end of a farm track, hidden behind a copse of trees. They had walked past it along the road to and from the beach many times and never realised it was there.

'Shoes off at the door,' he ordered, kicking off his own boots and disappearing inside, followed by his dogs. They did as they were told then trooped silently up the steps. The van was warm and dim, lit only by the flickering orange glow coming from a small, wood-burning stove. There was an over-whelming smell of dog. The space was divided into two sections, a larger living and sleeping area to the left and a small kitchen to the right. The dogs were in the living area, lined up in front of the stove and worshipping the flames which danced behind the glass window in the door. Dog Boy was in the kitchen, filling a kettle from a plastic water barrel.

'Go on. Go and get warm,' he said. 'Sit on the bed. There's nowhere else.'

They hesitated, glancing warily at the dogs, but the warmth coming from the stove was too tempting and they shuffled into the living area. The dogs looked up at them with soft eyes and thumped their tails on the floor once or twice, then went back to adoring the flames.

'Cosy,' said Frankie, beginning to relax a little.

'Thanks,' said Dog Boy, filling a tin tray with cups.

They sat down in a row on the bed, which was narrow but surprisingly comfortable. The wall behind the bed was covered with a padded back rest and, one by one, they let themselves lean back against it. The stove ticked, the gas hissed under the kettle and the dogs panted at their feet. The nightmare in the dunes seemed a world away.

'So,' said David, making himself sit up straight again. 'What should we call you?'

Dog Boy shrugged. 'You don't have to call me anything.'

'But everyone has a name,' persisted David. 'And we can't keep calling you Dog Boy.'

'Why not?'

'Well,' floundered David. 'It doesn't seem polite. You're older than us. You must be – what – twenty? We shouldn't be calling you Dog Boy.'

Dog Boy shrugged again. 'It's as good as any other label.'

David folded his arms and glared at the sleeping dogs. Dog Boy shook his head and smiled, then struck a match and held it up to the gas light on the wall until the mantle popped. A gentle, creamy light filled the van and suddenly they could see beyond the glow of the stove. Michael blinked and gazed around in astonishment. Every bit of the floor, the walls and the ceiling were covered with a patchwork of assorted carpet pieces, fitted neatly together like a furry jigsaw.

I could live like this, thought Michael, settling back onto the bed. *If things got too bad with Dad, I could do this*. He studied the van closely, imagining himself tucked up in the little bed or cooking his breakfast in the tiny kitchen.

'It's not all cosy firelight and cups of tea,' said Dog Boy, staring straight at Michael as though he had read his mind. 'It's freezing in winter. That's what the carpet's for – a bit of insulation.'

Michael blushed and took a mug of tea from the tray. Taking the last mug for himself, Dog Boy stood the tray against the wall and settled himself on the floor next to the dogs.

'Eeuuww! Gross!' grimaced Frankie, after her first sip.

'Drink it,' ordered Dog Boy. 'It's what you have after a shock – strong tea with lots of sugar.'

'Why?' demanded Frankie.

Dog Boy hesitated then scowled at Frankie. 'It's traditional.'

Frankie subsided, muttering, but she took a few more sips and was surprised to find that she was beginning to feel stronger and less shaky. The others were drinking too, except for David who was staring at the chipped rim of his mug with an expression of distaste on his face.

'So,' said David. 'Are you going to tell us what happened with your dogs?'

Dog Boy stretched out on the floor, using Daisy as a head rest. 'First, you tell me what you were doing there.'

Michael and Alice glanced at one another and then haltingly began to talk, telling the story between them. Dog Boy listened quietly, nodding encouragingly and ignoring David's impatient sighs.

He stopped them only once, when Alice was describing the energy that had flowed through the dune hollow that afternoon.

'Tell me what he said, again,' interrupted Dog Boy.

Alice looked confused for a moment. She had been lost in her story. 'Who, Michael? Um – he said, "I think we woke something up".'

'What did you mean by that?' asked Dog Boy, training his strange, blue and green gaze on Michael.

Michael shrugged. 'I can't even remember saying it.'

Dog Boy studied him for a few seconds longer, then nodded at them to continue. He listened quietly again until they got to the part where the dune slope had collapsed, burying David. Frankie was joining in by this time, adding her own, special gory details. She was really getting into describing the moment when David's hand had come clawing out of the sand when she noticed that Dog Boy was sitting bolt upright, staring at David as though he could not quite believe his eyes.

'What?' said Frankie, annoyed at having to stop in mid-flow.

'Yeah, what?' repeated David, glowering at Dog Boy.

'You don't know how lucky you are,' breathed Dog Boy.

'Yeah, well I don't feel that lucky,' muttered David, easing his sandy collar away from his neck. 'And I'm still waiting to hear—'

'—what happened,' finished Dog Boy, with a suggestion of irritation in his voice. 'I know.' He put down his empty mug and took a deep breath. 'O.K. First off, the child in the dune. It's not a little girl. It's a little boy.'

'But – she had long hair, in a plait,' said Alice.

'He,' corrected Dog Boy. 'His hair is plaited the way Celtic men and boys used to wear their hair. And did you see that thick sort of paste covering the plait? That's a lime wash. They used to put it on to make their hair go blonder.'

'Did you say Celtic?' asked Michael. 'That was a long time ago, wasn't it? How long has he been in that box?'

'About two thousand years,' said Dog Boy, and Michael shuddered. 'I think that little boy was an Iron Age Celt.'

'Thank you, Indiana Jones,' muttered David.

Dog Boy gazed at him calmly. 'You are a one for the labels, aren't you?'

'David's only wondering how you know these things,' said Alice, loyally.

'I know because I spent the whole of last summer working at Miltown Living Village.'

'Milwhat?' asked Frankie.

'Oh, I know that place!' said Michael. 'It's about twenty miles inland from here. I went out there once, to have a look around. It was really interesting. They reconstructed a Celtic village and there were people dressed like Celts, living in the huts and cooking their food on open fires and stuff.'

'Yeah, that's the place,' said Dog Boy. 'We all had to stay in character once we were in our costumes. I was supposed to be a vassal, working for the local landowner. That's like one step away from slavery.

Vassals were free men but it didn't count for much because they had no money and nowhere else to go.

'I think that boy might have been a vassal, too. Or even a slave. He's dressed just the same as they dressed me at Miltown. Nothing fancy, just a basic woollen tunic and a cloak. Poor kid . . .'

Dog Boy trailed off and frowned into the fire.

'Why do you say that?' asked Alice.

'I think he was a sacrifice,' said Dog Boy, simply.

Michael went pale. 'I knew it,' he whispered. 'He was alive when they put him in there . . .'

'That's rubbish, Michael!' shouted David, jumping to his feet. 'He died and they sealed him in the box with a load of salt to preserve the body. It's the most obvious explanation.'

Dog Boy was shaking his head. 'Salt was very valuable back in those times. I don't think they would have wasted it on a vassal or a slave boy.'

'That's only your opinion,' said David. 'You can't prove anything. You don't know the facts.'

'I tell you what,' said Dog Boy. 'Why don't you sit down and be quiet for five minutes?'

David looked as though he was going to argue, but Dog Boy stared at him with a cold blue and green gaze and he sat back down on the bed without saying anything more.

'You want facts,' said Dog Boy. 'I can give you facts if that helps. The Iron Age Celts weren't really into mummification. They weren't even into burial unless it was someone important. Most of them were cremated when they died – and only the lucky ones got their ashes put into a pot. What the Celts were into in a big way was human sacrifice – and yes, I can

69

prove it,' he added as David started to say something. 'Have you heard of the bog bodies?'

Michael nodded. 'The bodies survived because there's something in the bog water that preserves them.'

'Tannic acid,' said Dog Boy.

'That's it. I remember seeing this programme about a woman's body they found in a bog in Wales, back in the 1960s. They started a full murder investigation and then this expert came along and told them she was thousands of years old.'

'And why did they start a murder investigation?'

'Because . . .' Michael paused and turned to stare at Dog Boy, his face full of a sudden understanding. 'Because her throat had been cut.'

'So far over two hundred bog bodies have been uncovered in Britain. They all died roughly two thousand years ago and they didn't all just happen to fall into a bog and drown. Nearly all of them died violently. Some were garotted, some had their throats cut and some were pinned down in the bog with stakes. They were taken to the bogs and offered as ritual sacrifices to Celtic gods.'

'Hang on a minute,' said Alice. 'None of that happened to the little boy in the dune. That box was built into the wall of a house—'

'Not a house,' said Dog Boy. 'Iron Age huts were made of wood or mud with turfs or thatch on the roof. I'm sure that curved stone wall must be part of an early lime kiln. I think there was a working community in the dunes in Iron Age times, quarrying for lime and probably evaporating salt out of sea water as well. I think, maybe, when they built that kiln, they made a gift of salt to one of their gods, to bring luck to the kiln, and they thought they'd throw in that little boy, too. Just as an afterthought. He was probably worth a lot less than the salt to them.'

'But you can't prove it—' began David.

'No, I can't prove it,' flared Dog Boy. 'I'm guessing now, O.K.? I'm all out of facts.'

'Yes, well, that was all very interesting,' said David, in a bored voice. 'But none of it explains what happened with your dogs on the beach, does it?'

For the first time Dog Boy looked unsure of himself. 'No,' he muttered. He turned away and concentrated on scratching Daisy behind the ear.

'So,' said Frankie. 'Explain.'

'O.K. But something tells me that logic-boy over there is going to flip.'

'Try me,' said David.

Dog Boy sighed, then he ducked his head and began to talk, fast and low. 'I think there is something that – lives – on that stretch of the beach. It's something very old and very bad. I don't know what it is. I don't even know whether living is the right word for what it does. The Celts might have called it a god – some of their gods were pretty nasty. Whatever it is, it likes death. It likes sacrifices. And somewhere along the line it developed a taste for little boys.'

There was a shocked silence. David was staring at Dog Boy in total disbelief but Michael and Alice exchanged a frightened glance. They had both been in the hollow that afternoon and what Dog Boy was saying now made a strange sort of sense. Michael glanced at the caravan door, imagining the fog swirling outside in the fading light. Suddenly, the catch holding the door shut looked very flimsy to him.

'Excuse me?' said Frankie. 'Did you say little boys?'

'The little lad in the stone box, he's not the only boy to die on that beach, although he must have been one of the first. There have been other deaths since.'

'Nah. I don't buy it,' said Frankie. 'If all these little boys have been dying, how come we haven't heard about it? How come all the parents aren't telling their kids to stay away from the beach?'

'Because people have very short memories,' said Dog Boy. 'And sometimes there are more than a hundred years between the deaths on the beach. But there are two things which link all the deaths. The boys all suffocated—'

'Like the boy in the box,' whispered Michael, remembering how he ran out of air in his nightmare.

'—and each time a boy died, it happened just after the ground had been disturbed on that particular stretch of beach.'

'You think we woke something up this afternoon,' said Michael, flatly.

Dog Boy nodded. 'And it's hungry again.'

David burst out laughing. 'That's the trouble with little boys. You eat one and, a hundred years later, you want another one. They're so more-ish, aren't they?'

'I don't know why you're laughing,' snapped Dog Boy. 'You were very nearly its latest meal.'

David stopped laughing and stared at Dog Boy. 'You really believe all this, don't you? Look, that dune collapsed on me this evening because we were stupid enough to undermine it when we dug the hole. That's all. No mysterious bad thing, just bad engineering.'

'And the wolves we all saw this evening? You can't put that down to bad engineering. My dogs don't make a habit of shape-shifting – they're perfectly happy in their own skins.'

David scowled. He had been trying to puzzle that one out ever since they arrived at the caravan, but he still could not explain the wolves and that made him angry. He stood up and folded his arms. 'Go on then,' he shot back at Dog Boy. 'You explain it. You said you could.'

'I could, but you won't like it.'

David shrugged. 'Nothing new there, then.'

'David!' said Alice, warningly.

'Well, it's all such rubbish—'

'You haven't heard it yet,' said Alice, giving him a look. David sighed and sat down again, perching on the very edge of the bed.

'I've done some research into all this,' continued Dog Boy. 'Celtic myths and legends are full of stories about shape-shifting. They believed that their gods could change shape into hares or crows, or even take possession of a human body. They thought that the spirit of a dead person could possess the living, too. Spirits had to be appeased, otherwise they could become spiteful and destructive.'

'But they're just stories,' protested Alice.

'Yes but where did the stories come from? If this

thing was there two thousand years ago – and I think it was – they would have called it a god. That's how they would've explained it.'

'And you think it can shape-shift?' asked Frankie.

'No. I think it can get inside our heads and make us see things that aren't there. Like dogs turning into wolves, for instance. And think about what happened to you this afternoon.' Dog Boy looked at Michael. 'You thought you were suffocating in a stone box. You believed it so strongly, you actually stopped breathing.'

Michael and Alice shared another frightened look. Michael was remembering how real his nightmare had been. Alice was thinking about the few minutes when Michael had turned into someone else.

'Right. That's it,' said David, breaking the spell. 'I've heard enough. I'm leaving.'

'Bye then,' said Dog Boy.

David blinked with surprise. 'Right,' he said, and hesitated.

'Go on, then,' said Dog Boy. 'There's no point in staying. You're not listening.'

David stood up and looked at the others. 'Let's go.'

Alice, Michael and Frankie got to their feet reluctantly, sending scared glances towards the caravan door. Dog Boy stood up too . 'I'll walk you into town if you like,' he offered. The dogs heard the magic word 'walk' and raced to the door, nearly knocking David over.

'We don't need an escort!' he yelled, pushing his way through the dogs to the door. He twisted the catch and the door swung outwards, hitting the wall of the caravan with a hollow thud. The dogs shot out and disappeared into the haar. David hesitated again, peering out into the dense fog.

'What are you waiting for?' said Dog Boy. 'It's all rubbish, remember?'

'Don't,' pleaded Alice, staring at the tendrils of fog creeping across the floor of the caravan.

'You'll be all right,' said Dog Boy, relenting. 'As long as you don't go back to the beach.'

Michael drew a sharp breath as he suddenly realised something. 'But the summer holidays have started! The beach is going to be heaving with kids.'

Alice's eyes widened. 'My brothers are having their birthday party there on Sunday . . .'

She stared at Dog Boy and Dog Boy stared back bleakly, then rubbed his hand over his eyes. 'Well, maybe it's all over for now. Maybe that thing lost its appetite after it tried to swallow logic-boy over there.'

'Stop calling me that!' yelled David. 'And you two,' he added, glaring at Alice and Michael, 'stop acting as though it's all true! He hasn't given you a shred of proof—'

David stopped as Dog Boy yanked open a drawer and pulled out a cardboard folder. 'Here,' he said, taking a yellowing newspaper cutting from the folder and holding it out to them. 'That happened ten years ago.'

Alice took the cutting and held it so that they could all see it. David stepped away from the door and looked over her shoulder. 'It's from the local paper,' said Alice, looking at the top of the page.

' "Boy buried under collapsing dune . . ." Oh, David. That could have been you.'

'Let me see,' said Frankie, snatching the cutting. ' "A verdict of accidental death has been reached in the tragic case of a young holiday-maker who was suffocated when the dune he was digging into collapsed and buried him. The boy's brother managed to dig him out but was too late to save him." Man,' she breathed, handing the cutting back to Dog Boy. 'That must've been tough on the brother.'

'Proof enough?' asked Dog Boy, slotting the cutting back into the folder.

'One boy,' said David. 'One accidental death. Is that all you've got?'

'No. You've heard of Philadelphia village? The one in the dunes?'

'Yes,' said David. 'Everybody knows about Philadelphia.'

'Do you know why the village died?'

'Yes,' said David with exaggerated patience. 'The market for lime collapsed when cement came on the scene. The quarry went out of business. The workers left.'

'That's the official story,' said Dog Boy. 'But there is another version. There's an old guy who always sits on that bench down at the harbour-end on sunny days—'

'—with the flat cap and the walking stick,' said Michael.

'That's him,' said Dog Boy. 'He's called George. George can tell you a different story about Philadelphia village.'

'Stories again,' muttered David.

'When George's father was a little boy, he lived in Philadelphia village,' continued Dog Boy, pointedly ignoring David. 'He lived there because his dad – George's grandad – worked in the lime quarries. One day they started quarrying in a new part of the dunes – no prizes for guessing where – and they dug up an old wooden box and inside it they found—'

'—severed heads,' sighed David. 'We know. And there was gold there too. It's just another story!'

'No. George said there was no gold. His grandad was there when they found the box. There was no gold, only heads.'

'So where is it?' demanded David. 'If they found a box as old as that, then why isn't it in the museum? Why . . .?' David stopped talking, then began to smile as an idea came to him.

Dog Boy did not notice the smile. 'The point is,' he continued, 'even though George's grandad swore there was no gold in the box, the rumours started up and grew into a sort of gold fever. Philadelphia was a tight-knit community before they found the box. Afterwards, everybody was suspicious of everybody else. People would go off on their own, digging for gold and, while they were gone, other folk would search their cottages! Things got worse and worse and, even before the tragedy, people were starting to leave.'

'What tragedy?' asked Frankie, already half-knowing the answer.

'One of the villagers had dug this tunnel right into the side of the dune and he was sure he could see something gleaming right at the back, but he couldn't reach it. He came running back to the village and grabbed two of George's dad's friends and he made these two kids go into the tunnel.'

'And the tunnel collapsed on them,' said Alice, feeling icy fingers trace their cold way down her spine.

'Two families lost their sons,' said Dog Boy. 'That was the end of the village.' He looked over at David, expecting another argument, but David was leaning against the wall of the caravan, smiling.

'What?' said Dog Boy, suspiciously.

'I don't know why I didn't think of it before,' smiled David, looking at Alice, Frankie and Michael. 'It was when I mentioned the museum back there – it gave me an idea. All we have to do is to go to the curator and tell him what we found! He'll sort it all out from there.'

Dog Boy slammed his fist against the caravan wall. 'Have you not heard a word I've said? That is the very last thing we want right now!'

'Why not?' asked Frankie. 'It sounds like a good idea to me. Bring the experts in. Within a week we'll know everything there is to know about that poor kid in the dune. I bet they can even find out what he had for his last breakfast.'

'Listen to me,' said Dog Boy, unclenching his fists and making a great effort to stay calm. 'If you tell the museum guy, he'll bring in the archaeologists and they'll start digging holes for all they're worth. Next thing you know, the dunes'll be swarming with kids come to watch the show. We have to keep this quiet—'

'No way,' said David. 'I'm going to the museum tomorrow and you can't stop me.'

Dog Boy finally snapped. He lunged forward, grabbed David by the shoulders and flung him out through the caravan door. David staggered down the metal steps and fell over in the mud.

'Hey!' said Frankie, putting her hands on her hips and glaring at Dog Boy. He glared back at her with eyes like chips of blue and green glass.

'Out,' he grated. 'All of you, out!'

As they hurried down the steps, Dog Boy gave a piercing whistle and the three dogs pelted out of the fog and into the caravan. Alice and Michael bent to help David to his feet and the door banged shut behind them.

'I've been thrown out of better places than this!' yelled Frankie, but there was no answer. Dog Boy had abandoned them to the fog. They were going to have to make their own way home.

7

'That was some scary walk home,' said Frankie the next day as they sat in their favourite fish and chip shop, eating lunch. 'It all seems a lot less scary now the sun's shining again. Isn't it glorious? I'm wearing my new summer outfit, guys. Did you notice?'

'Very nice,' grunted David, barely glancing at Frankie's orange top and lime green shorts.

'As for you, Alice,' said Frankie, with a disapproving sigh. 'You look like you're still expecting fog.'

Alice looked down at her usual faded T-shirt and jeans then gave Frankie an embarrassed smile.

'Everybody's real talkative today,' commented Frankie. 'I guess we're still recovering from last night. We all got into quite a state, what with the fog and Dog Boy's weird stories.'

'Don't talk to me about that idiot,' growled David.

'I nearly wet myself when that cat jumped out of the tree,' continued Frankie, completely ignoring David. 'I didn't sleep a wink all night.'

'It doesn't seem to have spoiled your appetite,' commented Michael, watching Frankie spear four large chips with her fork and shovel them into her mouth.

'Hey, you know me and food,' grinned Frankie,

giving Michael a good view of a mouthful of chewed-up chips. Michael grimaced and pushed his own plate of chips away from him. Alice studied his face with a worried frown. He was very pale with dark circles under his eyes.

'Not hungry, Michael?' asked Frankie, hooking the nearly full plate towards her.

'Frankie!' said Alice.

'What?'

'You hated chip-shop chips when you first came over here. Now you eat too many of the things.' Alice rescued the plate and pushed it back to Michael.

'I burn it all off,' protested Frankie. 'I've been on these all morning.' She lifted one leg and rested a roller-booted foot on the edge of the table.

'But your mum flew in from America early this morning, didn't she?' said Alice. 'I thought you'd be spending some time with her. You haven't seen her since Easter.'

'I know,' said Frankie, eyeing up Michael's bread. 'But she was tired and travel sick. She barfed up in the kitchen sink. It was gross! She went to bed to sleep it off.'

'What about you, Michael?' asked Alice. 'How did you sleep?'

Michael shrugged. 'I had stuff on my mind.'

'Did your dad give you a hard time for staying out all evening?'

'I wish he had,' said Michael. 'It would've been better than the silent treatment.'

'Awww! He's not still into that, is he?' said Frankie. 'How long is it now?'

'Three months,' said Michael, softly, rubbing his forehead.

'And all because you told him you wanted to spend more time with your friends?'

'He says if I want to run my life then he's not going to interfere in any way. So, he doesn't ask me where I'm going. He doesn't tell me where he's going. He leaves meals under a plate for me to heat up. It's . . . horrible. But I'm not going back to how it was, with him controlling every minute of my day. I'm not giving in.'

'Man, he is one weird guy.'

'He's not!' said Michael, hotly.

'O.K.! Don't bite my head off!'

'Sorry. I mean . . . look, Frankie – it's complicated. He wasn't always like this. It just sort of – crept up on him, especially after he lost his job. Being a father became the only job he had. He took it too far, that's all. Now I don't know how to put things right.'

'Hey! You're the kid. He's the grown up. It's up to him to put things right.'

Michael turned to gaze out the window. Frankie leaned forward and put her hand over his. 'Michael,' she said, seriously.

'What?'

'Can I have your chips?'

'Frankie!' began Alice, but Michael was spluttering with surprised laughter and Frankie was joining in. The laughter grew and soon they were leaning their heads together and flapping their hands at one another weakly, trying to call a halt. Alice sat back in her chair and shook her head, but she was grinning despite herself.

'Are they crazy or what?' she asked, turning to David.

'Hmmm?' David turned his blue eyes Alice's way, but he wasn't really looking at her. His thoughts were somewhere else.

'I said – oh, never mind. Are you going to sit there and say nothing all through lunch?'

'I'll talk,' said David, 'when we get onto the serious stuff. I thought the idea was to come here before we go over to the museum, so we can work out what to say to the curator?'

Frankie and Michael stopped laughing and they all looked out across the sunny square to the imposing pillared front of the town museum.

'I don't know whether we should say anything,' said Michael, slowly. 'I was thinking, what if Dog Boy is right? What if we should be keeping people out of the dunes, not sending them in there?'

'Come on!' said David. 'We can't listen to him. He's a – a waster. He hasn't even got a proper job. He hasn't even got a proper name!'

'Still sore about getting chucked out into a muddy field?' asked Frankie.

'That muddy field belongs to Bill Armstrong,' said David. 'I'm going to check with Bill, next time I see him. I'm going to make sure he knows there's a ratty old van squatting there. If Bill's not careful, he'll have a field full of ratty old vans by the end of the summer.'

'Now that's a real nice way to repay Dog Boy's hospitality,' said Frankie, lazily. 'He is not a waster. Stop blindsiding him, Davey.'

'I'm not!' said David. '—What's blindsiding?'

'My dad says everybody's heart has a blind side to it,' explained Frankie. 'Some people's hearts have very tiny blind sides and some people's blind sides are ginormous! How wide your blind side is, that depends on what sort of shape your heart's been knocked into. Now you, Davey-boy, your heart's got a blind side this wide against people like Dog Boy. People who choose to live differently.'

David looked offended. 'Yes, but—'

'It's O.K.' said Frankie, kindly. 'You can't help it. It's the way you've been brought up. It's the shape your heart's been knocked into. D'you get me?'

'—um—'

'See, I know about this. Lots of people have got blind sides to their hearts where me and my mom and dad are concerned, because of the colour of our skin. Dad says to ignore them. He says they can't help it and they do more harm to themselves than to us.' Frankie stopped and looked David right in the eye. 'And right now, that's the problem you've got.'

'Problem . . .?'

'You're acting nasty. You're thinking nasty. You're harming yourself more than you're harming him. You won't listen to what he's saying because of who he is. But what if he's right, Davey?'

Alice and Michael stared at Frankie in surprise. One minute she was fooling around, being selfish and irritating – the next minute she came out with something amazing.

'I am going to miss you,' said Alice, softly.

'Yeah, well . . .' Frankie smiled and then shrugged, feeling an odd mixture of pleasure and sadness.

'Does that mean you're agreeing with her?' said David, uncertainly.

'Well . . .'

'You are!'

'So,' said Frankie. 'Here's what I think we should do. It's kinda like a compromise. I think we should go over to the museum and find out as much as we can from this curator guy without telling him about the boy in the dune. Not yet, anyway. We pretend we're doing a project on mummies and we ask a load of questions – and then we can decide for ourselves what's the best thing to do.'

David opened his mouth to object, then shut it again. He had to admit that Frankie had come up with a good plan. He pushed his chair back and stood up. 'Let's go, then,' he said.

The museum was dark and chilly after the bright sunshine outside. They moved through the cavernous ground-floor rooms and the sound of their footsteps floated up to the high ceilings then bounced back to them.

'Looks like we got the place to ourselves,' said Frankie, skating across the polished marble floor and executing a neat turn round a bust of Queen Victoria on a plinth. The wheels on her roller boots rumbled loudly as she zig-zagged between a long row of glass display cases.

'So, how do we find the curator?' asked Alice, scanning the empty room.

'I'll go back to the reception desk,' offered Michael. 'Maybe there's a bell or something.'

'Eeeuuuwww!' shrieked Frankie, before he could make a move. 'Come and look at this!'

They hurried over to Frankie, who was staring into the last display case in the row. It contained a collection of items salvaged from an old shipwreck off the coast. Most of it was the usual odd assortment of coins and jewellery and old-fashioned spectacles, but Frankie was staring at something on a blue velvet cushion, right in the middle of the case. It was a tiny, shrivelled black hand with a polished brass cuff covering the amputation site.

' "A monkey's paw, found in a lead-lined box" ' read David, peering at the card beside the cushion. ' "Believed to be a good luck charm." '

'It didn't bring them much luck,' said Michael, making Frankie snigger beside him.

'I think it's awful,' said Alice, gazing at the little hand. It made her think of the shrivelled hands of the little boy in the dunes. 'You know what it reminds me of?'

'What does it remind you of?' said a deep voice from the other side of the case.

Alice looked up and jumped as she saw a distorted face staring at her through two panes of glass. The dark eyes watching her looked huge and fish-like. Hastily she stood up and the man on the other side of the case straightened up too.

'James Nardini, the new museum curator,' he said, holding out his hand across the top of the case. He was young and handsome, with thick black hair and brown eyes which twinkled at her, but Alice reached out and took his hand reluctantly. She could not rid herself of that first image of him, mouthing at her through the distorted glass like some cold thing from the bottom of the sea. She shook his hand gingerly and tried to let go, but he held on for an instant.

'What does it remind you of?' he repeated, nodding down at the monkey paw beneath their clasped hands.

Alice tried to think of an answer, but her mind went blank. 'Nothing,' she said, lamely.

'Well,' said James Nardini, solemnly, releasing her hand to shake hands with David, Frankie and Michael in turn. 'Welcome to the museum. If there's anything I can help you with, anything at all . . .?'

He waited for a moment, eyebrows raised enquiringly. Alice and Michael both hesitated and looked at one another. Michael found that he was reluctant to say anything to this kind, twinkly-eyed man who could move so soundlessly across the marble floor in his suede shoes. There was something about the thick black hair and the soft, black designer suit which gave Michael the creeps.

David was the one who finally spoke. 'We're interested in burial practices. Mummies and stuff.'

'Mummies?' said James Nardini. 'That's not a school project, is it? I know all about them. Kathy – I mean Miss Broadbent, your history teacher and I, we work together very closely on the school projects.'

'I'll bet they do,' muttered Frankie to Alice, under her breath.

'Pardon?' said the curator.

'Nope. It's not a school project,' said Frankie. 'We're just kinda interested.'

'Now, why is it that children are always so fascinated with mummies?' said James Nardini, his eyes twinkling.

'Beats me, James,' said Frankie, zig-zagging off between the display cases again.

'Yes . . .' said the curator, his smile slipping slightly as he watched her skate back to him. 'And you are . . .?'

'Frankie.'

'Well, Frankie. Perhaps you should take those off in here. For your own safety. I wouldn't want you to fall through a display case or something . . .'

'O.K. Sure,' said Frankie, squatting down to unfasten the boots.

'So, can you help us?' asked David.

'It just so happens,' said the curator, turning his beaming smile back to full power, 'That burial practices are a bit of a speciality of mine. So, ask away!'

'Right. Can you mummify a body by putting it in a load of salt?'

'Well, the Egyptians used natron – that's a sort of salt.'

'No, we mean ordinary salt, like you put on your chips,' said Frankie, standing up again with her boots slung over her shoulder.

The curator shook his head, doubtfully. 'I've never heard of it. It might work, if the body was properly prepared.'

'Prepared?' asked David.

'The way the Egyptians did it. Removing the brains and internal organs . . . packing the cavities with—'

'But what if the body was just put in a box with a load of salt?' interrupted Frankie.

'No,' said the curator, decisively. 'That would

88

never work. Think about how much fluid there is in a body.'

'Even a little one?' asked Frankie.

'Oh, yes. The body would start to decompose and all the bodily fluids would leak out into the box. The salt would dissolve, making a sort of brine and then—'

'O.K.' said Frankie hurriedly, as her stomach lurched. 'We get the picture.'

David was looking grim. Everything he had heard so far went against his theory that the little boy in the dunes had been mummified deliberately. 'But, what if a body was put in a box with a load of salt and then sort of baked.'

'Baked?' said the curator, looking astonished. 'Baked in what?'

David was beginning to get embarrassed but he kept going, trying to describe the location of the box without mentioning lime kilns. 'Somewhere very hot, really hot – and dry – with lots of hot air . . .'

'Ah!' the curator's face cleared. 'Dry, hot conditions. I think we might be talking natural mummification here – but I don't know where salt would come into it.'

'Yeah, forget the salt,' said Frankie. 'Stupid idea. Salt! Sheesh!' She rolled her eyes and tutted contemptuously.

'Right. Well, there's a mummy in the British Museum which is nearly four thousand years old. It was found buried in the sand in the Egyptian desert. No natron. No organ removal. It dried out naturally, you see? Dry, hot conditions will do that. Even in this country, if you knock down an old house, you usually find something in the chimney – birds, mice, even the odd cat that got stuck up there. All beautifully mummified because of the—'

'—hot, dry conditions,' finished Frankie. 'In chimneys,' she added, giving David a meaningful look.

'Talking about this country,' said David, ignoring Frankie. 'Did they used to bury people in stone coffins?'

'What period in history are we talking about?'

'Oh, say . . . Iron Age?'

'They did, but it was very rare. Only very rich or very important people could afford it – a bit like mummification in Egypt. The best find we've had from that time is the stone tomb of a Celtic prince. He must have been very important.'

'How could you tell?'

'By the richness of the grave goods. He was surrounded by flowers and the tomb was packed with everything he might want or need in the next life. Bronze goods, badger hides, fish hooks, food and mead, gold brooches, plates, pots – even a pair of iron nail clippers!'

James Nardini stopped talking and gave David a searching look. 'These are very specific questions you're asking. Can I ask why you want to know these things?'

'Just curious,' said David, hurriedly. 'Really. Thanks very much.' He looked at the others and they all began moving towards the entrance. The curator let them go and David was just beginning to relax when Frankie stopped and turned back.

'Just one more thing,' she said, remembering Dog

Boy's story about the severed heads. 'How far back do the museum records go?'

'Right back to the day it opened,' said the curator. He nodded towards the bust of Queen Victoria. 'She cut the ribbon. There's an account of it at the start of the first record book. They're all in my office,' he said, pointing to a door at the back of the room. 'Are you wanting to look up anything in particular?'

'Yeah. There's a story about some severed heads being found in a box at Philadelphia Beach—'

'The beach?' said the curator, his eyes suddenly sharp with interest. He looked at the four of them more closely and his smile disappeared. 'I know who you are,' he said, softly. 'You were on the school trip yesterday, with Kathy, weren't you? She told me all about it.'

'Yeah, well if we could just have a look at those records,' said Frankie, trying to sound casual.

'No, I don't think so,' said James Nardini. 'They're for serious scholars only.' He stared at Michael. 'You're the one, aren't you? The boy who gave Kathy a black eye.'

'Sorry,' whispered Michael, heading for the door. 'I didn't mean to.'

'You've found something, haven't you?' said the curator, hurrying after them. 'On the beach.'

'No. We haven't found anything.'

'You've been digging in the dunes, haven't you?'

Frankie started to run and the others followed, racing towards the square of sunshine beyond the open museum door.

'Wait a minute!' shouted the curator, behind them. 'If you've found something of historical importance, you must hand it over to the authorities!'

Frankie shot out of the museum door and stumbled down the steps outside in her socks. 'Quick!' she shouted. 'This way!'

They pelted round the corner of the building and flattened themselves against the wall just as James Nardini appeared on the museum steps. Frankie eased round the corner again and hid behind a bush, watching the curator scan the square, looking for them. After a few minutes, he gave up and went back inside.

'He's gone,' said Frankie, turning back to the others.

Michael let the air out of his lungs and leaned back against the sunny wall. 'I didn't like him,' he said. 'He looked like a vampire.'

'Well done, Frankie,' said David, tightly. 'Great job back there.'

'Hey!' yelled Frankie. 'Get off my back!'

'What on earth were you trying to do?'

'It would've been the final proof,' said Frankie. 'You know? Those facts you're always droning on about? If some severed heads really were found at Philadelphia beach, it would be in the museum records. If the heads were real, the chances are the rest of Dog Boy's story is real, too. We'd have our proof. We'd know where we stand. That's what I was trying to do.' Frankie sighed and bent down to strap her roller boots back on.

'So what do we do now?' asked Alice.

Frankie straightened up and delivered one of her trade mark wicked grins. 'Well, I don't know about you guys, but I've decided what I'm going to do. I'm going back in to look at those record books.'

'Are you crazy?' gasped David.

'He was on his way out to lunch, when he stopped to talk to us,' said Frankie patiently. 'He had his jacket on and he was carrying his wallet. You watch, he'll be out again in a few minutes.'

Frankie was right. James Nardini came strolling out into the sunshine less than two minutes later.

'Not a vampire then,' said David, giving Michael a sideways glance.

'He's waiting for someone,' said Michael, watching the curator settle down on the museum steps.

'And here she comes,' said Alice, pointing across the square. Miss Broadbent was making her way towards the museum. She was wearing sunglasses with very large, mirrored lenses. James Nardini hurried over to Kathy Broadbent, removed her glasses and planted a tender kiss on her bruised cheek.

'Oh, Michael!' crowed Frankie. 'Look at that! What a shiner!'

They watched the couple move away across the square. 'O.K.' muttered Frankie. 'How about a nice, long pub meal? No, they've gone past the pub. Fish and chips, then, with ice cream to follow. No, they don't want that. They're headed for – the bakery?' Frankie flung herself against the wall and slid down into a crouch. 'What a cheapskate. He's going to buy her a measly sandwich!'

'That's that, then,' sighed David. 'We won't have enough time.'

'You know what?' said Frankie, a determined gleam lighting up her eyes. 'I'm still going in there.'

'You can't!' said Alice. 'It's too risky. They might take their sandwiches back to his office!'

'Or they might sit out in the square.' Frankie pushed herself upright. 'Anyway, what can he do if he catches me? Shoot me?'

Frankie looked over at the bakery. The couple were still inside. 'I'm doing it,' she said and disappeared round the corner before anyone could stop her. 'Somebody stand look-out!' she called over her shoulder as she skated up the wheelchair ramp and into the museum.

'Right,' said David. 'I'll go with her. Michael, you stand just inside the door and act as look-out. Alice, you wait outside the office and let us know when Michael gives the warning signal. Come on, then!'

David set off at a trot without looking back. Michael looked at Alice, his face pinched with fear. 'I'm scared,' he admitted.

'Join the club,' sighed Alice, turning to follow David.

'There's going to be trouble,' called Michael softly.

'Would you rather leave them in there on their own?' asked Alice, turning back.

Michael shook his head, took a deep breath and followed Alice into the museum.

8

Minutes later, Michael was standing in the shadows, just inside the museum entrance, peering across the square at the bakery and feeling as though his heart was about to explode right out of his chest. He glanced anxiously at Alice who stuck her head round the office door then turned back to Michael and gave a thumbs up.

'How did I get into this?' muttered Michael, turning back to watch the bakery.

In the office, Frankie and David had found the big, leather-bound record books on a shelf behind the curator's desk. David looked quickly along the spines and his heart sank. Each book covered a full decade of museum business.

'Which decade, Davey?' said Frankie, looking at him with bright-eyed expectation.

'This one,' said David, with much more confidence than he felt. Together, they lifted the heavy book from the shelf, placed it on the curator's desk and began to search through the closely written pages.

At the entrance, Michael stiffened. He had seen a movement in the doorway of the bakery. He screwed up his eyes, trying to get a better look, then his eyes widened and he took a step further back into the shadows. Miss Broadbent and James Nardini were coming out of the bakery.

'Don't panic,' breathed Michael, repeating David's last minute instructions. 'Just wait. They might sit in the square to eat.' He watched, holding his breath, as Miss Broadbent and James Nardini strolled across the square, passing one empty bench after another.

In the office, David was getting desperate. He and Frankie had raced through most of the record book, skimming page after page, but they had found nothing. Now they were getting near the end, he was sure they must have missed something. Reluctantly, he turned to Frankie. 'I think we might need to go back—' he began.

'No, look,' Frankie's eyes widened as she turned the next page. 'The handwriting's changed. It's a new guy starting from here. And look what he says!'

David followed Frankie's pointing finger and read out the first entry in the new handwriting.

' "I am honoured to become the new custodian of our noble town's history with only a few days notice, following Mr Cartwright's enforced resignation. I shall draw a veil over the Philadelphia incident and move on to more edifying matters . . ." '

'Quick!' hissed Frankie. 'Turn back! Let's see what this Cartwright guy got up to . . .'

At the door, Michael groaned quietly to himself. Miss Broadbent and James Nardini had just passed the last bench and were walking towards the museum steps, deep in conversation. There was no doubt about it, they were heading for the curator's office. He turned to Alice and drew his finger across his throat.

Frankie and David were poring over Mr Cartwright's last entry when Alice burst into the office.

'They're coming!' hissed Alice. 'Come on! You have to get out!'

'Just a mo,' muttered Frankie.

Alice glanced over her shoulder. Michael had retreated into the main room of the museum and was semaphoring frantically to her.

'We have to leave. Now!' hissed Alice, sticking her head back into the office.

'There!' said David, triumphantly, stabbing his finger at the page. 'The quarry workers brought the heads in to the museum, look, and – hang on a minute . . . he sold them! He sold them to a private collector. He says they were nasty, worthless objects that had no place in his museum. He swears there were no golden torcs in the box and he can't understand what all the fuss is about.'

Alice moaned quietly and looked back into the main room. For a second she thought Michael had run off and left them, then she saw his pale face watching her from the shadows. He had ducked down behind a large wooden chest of specimen drawers in the far corner of the room.

'Hurry!' he hissed, beckoning her over to his hiding place. Alice hesitated, glancing back into the office. David and Frankie were struggling to force the record book back into its slot on the tightly packed shelf.

'It won't go!' whispered Frankie. Alice thought about dashing in to help, but then her head snapped round as she heard Miss Broadbent's tinkling laughter right outside the entrance.

'David, Frankie, get out of there,' she ordered, without taking her eyes from the museum entrance. Her mouth went dry as two lengthening shadows stretched across the floor. 'They're here!' she whispered, and sprinted towards Michael just as Miss Broadbent and James Nardini stepped through the entrance hall and began walking towards her.

With a stifled squeak, Alice dived onto the marble floor and slid the rest of the way over to Michael on her belly. He grabbed her T-shirt and yanked her out of sight behind the chest, then they huddled together in the gloom, staring at one another as Miss Broadbent's heels clacked past.

'Did they get out?' mouthed Michael.

Alice shook her head. Michael's eyes widened so much they were almost round. Together, they eased along to the corner of the specimen box and peered out. Miss Broadbent and James Nardini had nearly reached the office.

'It's all very strange,' Miss Broadbent was saying. 'Michael Adams was digging in one of the dunes yesterday afternoon, but I don't think he found anything valuable.'

'Well they're up to something,' said the curator. 'They were asking about burials and grave goods. If there's something in those dunes, I want to be the finder. The prize shouldn't go to a bunch of kids who don't know the value of what they're looking at. I'm going to go to the beach and investigate. Want to come along?'

Miss Broadbent slipped her hand into his. 'I'll bring a picnic. It'll be romantic.'

James Nardini smiled down at Miss Broadbent.

'Come here,' he growled, pushing open his office door and pulling her in behind him.

Alice and Michael cringed, waiting for the shouts, but they heard nothing except giggles and romantic murmurs. They looked at one another in bewilderment for a few seconds.

'Where are they?' whispered Alice.

'Who knows,' said Michael. 'Let's get out of here.'

They clambered to their feet and began to tiptoe towards the door. They were halfway across the room, in full view, when Alice caught a movement out of the corner of her eye. Someone was coming out of the office. She froze and turned, desperately trying to think of an excuse for coming back into the museum, but it wasn't the curator in the office doorway, it was David and Frankie.

Alice and Michael watched as David and Frankie backed quietly out of the office. Frankie was balancing on the rubber toe stops of her roller boots, David was holding her steady and they were both staring into the office where the curator and Miss Broadbent were still murmuring and giggling. Ten agonisingly slow steps later, David decided they were far enough away from the office. He let go of Frankie's arm and ran for the door, waving Michael and Alice out ahead of him. Frankie gave them a few seconds, then put her head down and belted towards the entrance hall as fast as her roller boots would go.

'What's that rumbling noise?' said Miss Broadbent from the office. James Nardini sprinted to the door and stuck his head out. The bust of Queen Victoria was rocking gently on its plinth but otherwise the room was still and quiet.

'Strange,' he said, staring at the bust. He thought he caught a flash of orange and lime green, right in the corner of his eye, but when he looked in that direction, the entrance hall was empty.

'How come they didn't see you!' gasped Alice, as they collapsed onto the bench outside the baker's. 'We were sure they were going to catch you!'

'Oldest trick in the book,' panted David, grinning broadly. 'When he opened his office door, we stood behind it.'

'We waited until they were well into a clinch,' said Frankie. 'Then we just tiptoed away.' She began to giggle. 'Those guys were so busy kissing, we could've tap-danced out of there with sparklers sticking out of our ears.'

'I feel sick,' said Michael, holding his stomach and staring back at the museum entrance.

'You did great, Michael,' smiled Alice. 'We can all relax now.'

'No we can't,' said David, suddenly serious. 'We have to go back to the dune.'

'What!' shrieked Frankie. 'Are you crazy?'

'We'll be all right if we stick together. It's a sunny Saturday afternoon. There'll be other people down there.'

'But why do we have to go back at all?' pleaded Michael.

'Because . . .' David frowned down at his boots, then forced himself to admit that he had been wrong. 'Because it looks as though Dog Boy knew what he was talking about. The dunes are dangerous.'

'I must be dumb or something,' said Frankie. 'Doesn't that mean we should be staying away?'

'You heard them talking in the museum. Nardini is planning to do a bit of exploring – and he's going to take Miss Broadbent along with him.'

'So?' said Frankie. 'We can't stop them. The dunes are open to everyone.'

'I know we can't stop them. But I'm not sure how good a job Dog Boy did last night, covering up that box. It was foggy and we were all scared. I want to go back and check it over – hide any evidence of digging.'

Frankie blew the hair off her forehead and looked up into the cloudless blue sky. 'Alice?' she said.

Alice nodded reluctantly.

'Michael?'

'I suppose so. As long as we stay together and get out of there at the first sign of anything strange.'

'O.K. Davey,' said Frankie. 'It looks like we're all in.'

As they moved off through the square, heading for the beach road, Nigel Dunn and two of his friends stepped out of the doorway of the baker's shop.

'Her kid brothers were right,' said Nigel, staring down the road after Alice and the others. 'They've been digging in the dunes. And it sounds like they might have found something.'

Nigel dumped his half-eaten doughnut in a nearby bin and turned to his friends. 'Fancy a treasure hunt?'

The beach was busy with people enjoying the good weather. Frankie, David, Alice and Michael threaded

101

their way along the top of the dunes, looking out for trouble and jumping every time a child shrieked.

'Do they have to be so loud?' complained Frankie.

'They're enjoying themselves,' said Alice.

'Well, I'm glad someone is,' muttered Frankie, fastening her roller boots together by the straps and slinging them over her shoulder.

'There are so many of them,' said Michael, hopelessly, watching the children as they tumbled down the dune slopes. 'We can't keep an eye on them all.'

David hurried on towards the dune hollow where the box was buried. He was becoming more and more worried. Every hollow they passed had a family group camped in it. What if there was someone in that hollow? What if there were children digging in the sand with their plastic spades? He shuddered and lengthened his stride so that the others had to struggle to keep up.

'It's the next one,' panted Michael, spotting the car park behind the dunes.

David nodded grimly and ran to the top of the dune. He looked down into the hollow and breathed a sigh of relief. 'It's empty,' he said.

Alice frowned. 'But don't you find that odd?' she said. 'How come that one is empty when every other hollow along here is full of holiday-makers?'

'That's easy,' said Michael, bleakly. 'It's still got that bad feeling about it. I can feel it, even from up here.'

'I think it's just as well we came back,' said David, peering down into the hollow. 'I think some of that slope has collapsed again. We'll just do a quick patch-up job.'

'Very quick,' pleaded Michael.

They floundered down the slope into the hollow and the noise of the holiday-makers faded away above their heads. The sun still shone overhead but the bottom of the hollow had a cellar chill about it.

'No wonder there was no-one camped in this one,' shuddered Michael.

'That slippage is worse than I thought,' said David. 'Look, you can see a corner of the box there – and some of the kiln wall.'

He covered up the wall and started to cover the box, then stopped as a worrying idea wormed its way into his head. What if that wasn't just natural slippage? What if someone else had found the box?

'You know,' said David. 'I think we'd better have a quick check inside the box, just in case someone's been in there.'

'Yes,' said Alice. 'That's a very good idea.'

'Of course we should look in the box,' agreed Frankie, throwing her roller boots down in the sand. All of a sudden she was convinced that uncovering the box was the only reasonable thing to do.

'Absolutely,' nodded Michael. He seemed to have forgotten all about the bad feeling he had sensed at the top of the dune.

'Just to check,' said Frankie.

To check what? said a little voice in the back of her mind, but Frankie ignored the voice and set about helping the others to scrape the sand away from the broken front slab. David lifted the slab away and they all leaned forward to peer inside.

The boy was still crouched in the chilly darkness, with his head turned towards the hole in the box as though he was searching for air. They stared at him in silence for a few seconds, their faces solemn. His fate seemed all the more horrifying to them as they stood in the sunshine with a high, blue sky overhead. Alice felt tears pricking at her eyes again. David cleared his throat.

'It all seems in order,' he said, gruffly. Let's cover him up.' He hefted the slab and was poised to slip it back into place when Michael leaned forward, staring intently at something in the back corner of the box.

'Just a minute,' said Michael. 'There's something sticking out of the salt back there.'

'Where?'

Michael pointed. 'There, beside his foot.'

David peered into the dark box. 'It looks like a handle of some sort.'

'Let me,' said Michael, still staring intently into the box. He rolled up his sleeve and eased his arm past the boy's stick-like legs. He grimaced as his arm brushed against the yellow, papery skin, but then his hand was round the handle.

'Got it,' he gasped and began to pull it out the salt.

'Bait digging again?' called a voice directly above their heads.

'It's Nigel Dunn,' groaned Alice, squinting up at the top of the dune. 'And he's got two of his friends with him.'

'Quick!' hissed David. 'He can't see yet, the angle's wrong.'

Frankie leaped forward and pulled Michael away from the box by the back of his T-shirt. He rolled down to the bottom of the hollow, clutching the object from the box in one hand. David slammed the slab back into place, Alice pushed an armload of sand up the slope and Frankie patted it down.

'Good,' muttered David, then he lifted his head to stare up at Nigel and his friends. 'Just mucking about,' he called, climbing up the slope towards them.

'What did you find?' asked Nigel.

'Dead seagull,' said David. 'It was a bit smelly so we covered it up again.'

'What's he got?' said Nigel, jerking his chin at Michael, who was still kneeling in the bottom of the hollow, bent over the thing he had taken from the box.

'Oh, he wanted the skull,' said David, still climbing. 'For his collection. You know what he's like. A bit weird.' He reached the top of the dune and smiled up at Nigel. Nigel looked back at him and sneered.

'Good try,' he said. 'But no coconut.' He straight-armed David in the chest, catching him off-balance and sending him tumbling down the dune slope.

'Let me see that!' shouted Nigel, striding down the slope towards Michael.

'Get lost, Nigel,' said Alice, stepping in front of him. Nigel pushed her out of the way and she sat down hard on the sand.

'You creep!' yelled Frankie, jumping onto his back. Before she could get a proper grip, Nigel bucked and twisted at the same time. Frankie went flying off his back and slammed into the floor of the hollow with all the breath knocked out of her. She lay on her back, gasping for air and Nigel bent over her.

'Oh, poor Frankie,' he cooed. 'You look like you could do with a drink.'

Frankie squinted up at him with watering eyes. The sun was behind his head and she could see nothing more than a dark blob, but she knew what he was about to do. She had seen him do it to another boy at school. He was going to spit into her mouth. Frankie shut her mouth tightly and twisted her head to the side, waiting for the warm splatter of saliva to hit her cheek. Instead, she heard Nigel give a surprised grunt. Something heavy landed beside her head, showering her with sand. Frankie rolled out of the way just as Alice let out a terrified scream.

Frankie jumped to her feet and looked over at Alice to see what was wrong. Alice and David were both staring at a spot behind her with identical looks of horror on their faces. Frankie turned round. Her eyes widened and both hands went up to cover her mouth. Nigel was kneeling in the sand with his head thrown back at an unnatural angle. Michael was standing behind Nigel. He had one hand tangled in Nigel's hair, pulling his head back. The other hand was holding a knife to Nigel's exposed throat.

Frankie stared at the knife. It was crudely made of a dull, grey metal that had no shine to it. It looked heavy and too big for Michael's hand, but Michael was holding it with a sure confidence. The point was digging into the soft skin at the base of Nigel's throat. Nigel rolled his eyes their way and croaked. The knife point dug deeper into his throat. Nigel's hands fluttered briefly and he stiffened.

'Michael,' breathed Frankie, looking into his eyes. He stared back at her for a moment with a flat, silvery gaze that had no recognition in it, then he flexed his knife arm, preparing to cut Nigel's throat. There was a scuffle from the top of the dune as Nigel's friends turned and ran. Frankie covered her eyes.

'Space shuttle!' screamed Alice, suddenly. 'World wide web! Global warming! DVD's!'

David and Frankie stared at Alice as though she had gone mad, but Michael had cocked his head, listening. The hand holding the knife was still.

'—Premier League! Third World Debt – um – G.C.S.E.s . . .'

Alice glanced at Michael. The knife had dropped away from Nigel's throat and the hand in his hair had loosened its grip.

'—Theme Parks! Solar Power! Contact Lenses . . .'

Michael let go of Nigel's hair and stared down at the knife in his hand. Nigel scrambled to his feet, sobbing with fear and climbed unsteadily up the slope of the dune.

'Are you all right?' said David, reaching out to him.

'Get away from me!' yelled Nigel. He scrambled up to the top of the dune and sent one fearful look back at Michael. Then he wiped his face on his sleeve and ran off after his friends.

Down in the dune hollow, Michael suddenly flung the knife away from him and sat down. He was trembling all over. David picked up the knife and threw it out of Michael's reach.

'I didn't mean to do that,' whispered Michael. 'I didn't know I was doing that . . .'

'It's O.K.' said Alice, kneeling down and putting her arms round him. 'It wasn't you doing it.'

'How did you know that would work?' said David, looking at Alice with respect in his eyes.

'I didn't,' shrugged Alice. 'I just remembered the ball bouncing into the hollow last night. It made the wolves disappear – a little, rubber ball . . . It was something from our time, you see. I think that's what broke the spell.'

'So you just started yelling out every modern thing you could think of?'

Alice nodded and smoothed Michael's hair back from his forehead. 'Come on,' she said. 'Let's get him out of here.'

Alice and Frankie helped Michael out of the dune hollow while David retrieved the knife, carrying it by the very tip of the handle. They moved in silence through the laughing family groups and down to the edge of the sea. There, David pulled his arm back and threw the dagger as far as he could. It arced over and over then plunged into the sea with hardly a splash. They stood quietly for a moment, gazing at the spot where the dagger had disappeared and letting the sun warm them.

'Uh oh,' said David, looking over his shoulder. 'It's the beach patrol.'

They all looked round. Dog Boy was running towards them along the sand, with Daisy, Clem and Jet at his heels.

'What's going on?' panted Dog Boy, skidding to a halt beside them. 'There was this kid back there, running away from the dunes as though the devil was after him.'

'That was Nigel. Michael just tried to kill him with a knife,' said Frankie, matter-of-factly.

Michael winced and ran a trembling hand through his hair. 'It wasn't me,' he whispered.

'Anyway, Alice had this idea and—'

'Were you in the dune?' interrupted Dog Boy.

'Yes,' muttered David.

'That's where we found the knife,' explained Alice. 'It was in the box—'

'What!' Dog Boy stared at them accusingly. 'I tell you to keep away from the dunes and, not only do you go back, you dig up the box again! Are you mad!'

'Look, it wasn't like that—' began David.

'Some other kid just nearly died. What is it going to take for you idiots to believe me?'

'We believe you!' yelled David. 'That's why we came back. We wanted to make sure no one else would find it.'

Dog Boy shook his head, sending his dreadlocks flying. 'I'm keeping an eye on things. Why don't you kids just go home.'

'You can't order us about like we were your dogs,' flared David. 'Why should we trust you, anyway? How do we know you're not part of it? How come you know so much about it?'

'I told you, I've been looking into it.'

'But why?' demanded David. 'What made you start looking? What made you start finding out how many little boys had died here? That's a pretty sick interest if you ask me—'

'I was the brother,' said Dog Boy quietly.

'The brother?' repeated David.

'Ten years ago. The boy who died in the dunes. I was the brother. I was there when the dune collapsed on him. I dug him out, but I was too late. He was called Andrew . . .'

There was an uncomfortable silence. David looked down at his feet, then turned to Dog Boy. 'Sorry.'

'That's why I came back,' said Dog Boy, simply. 'I knew it wasn't an accident. I knew that ten years ago. I wanted to find out what killed him. I still do. So,' he said, turning to Michael, 'why don't we go and sit down over there and you can tell us about the knife.'

They settled on the warm sand and the dogs collapsed beside them. Michael sat for a moment, collecting his thoughts. 'It started as soon as I touched the handle,' he said and looked uncertainly at Alice.

'Go on,' said Alice, nodding encouragingly.

'I think I know what happened to the boy.' Michael stopped again, trying to make sense of the images which had filled his mind. The pictures had faded in and out like a badly cut film, and there were big gaps in the story.

'He was alive when he went into the box,' said Michael. 'But he wasn't a sacrifice. I saw him, running up to the kiln. He was holding a man's hand and he was scared – but not of the man. There were shouts and screams all around, people running. I think they were being attacked by raiders.' Michael looked questioningly at Dog Boy. 'Does that sound right?'

110

Dog Boy nodded. 'They were violent times. There was always the danger of a raid by another tribe. They were after salt, maybe, or slaves.'

'The man pulled a stone out of the side of the kiln, then he slid the top off the box hidden inside. He put his hands under the boy's arms and lifted him up. And it was as though I was the boy. I could feel him lifting me. His hands were strong but he was gentle.' Michael's eyes were distant as he remembered, letting himself be drawn deeper into the story.

'He lowered me into the box on top of the salt. It was cramped and hot in there and I didn't really want to go in, but he looked down at me, this man, and his eyes were full of love. I think,' Michael swallowed and his voice trembled. 'I think he was my father.

'We both knew about the salt. It was our secret. Why was it secret . . .?' Michael paused, running another loop of film through his mind. 'We were building up a secret store, that was it! We were taking a little bit of salt from each day's harvest. Stealing it, I suppose, from our master. We were going to leave when the box was full, and buy a piece of land in another part of the country. My father had built the box into the kiln. He said it would keep the salt dry and good.'

Michael stopped and rubbed at the sudden goose-flesh on his arms. The next bit of the story was hard to tell.

'My father lifted the stone lid of the box and began to slide it into place. I started to cry. He looked down into the box and spoke to me and it was in a language I couldn't understand, but I knew what he was saying. He told me it was only for a while, until the

111

raiders had gone. He said the box would keep his two most precious things safe. Then he handed his dagger down to me and told me to protect myself if anyone found me before he came back to get me out. But he didn't come back. He didn't come back . . .'

Dog Boy nodded. 'Killed in the raid by the sound of it. Chances are one of the heads in the box was his. The Celts had a nasty habit of preserving the heads of defeated enemies.'

'For trophies?' asked David.

'A bit more than that,' said Dog Boy. 'It was another of their sacrificial rituals to their gods.'

'Do you remember anything else, Michael?' asked Alice, softly.

'I tried to move the stone lid but it was jammed into place. I shouted and screamed, but no-one came. Then it started to get so hot and I couldn't breathe and I . . .'

Michael stopped and looked at them, his eyes full of a bewildered hurt. 'And then I woke up in the dune, holding a knife to Nigel Dunn's throat.'

Everyone was quiet for a while, thinking about the little Celtic boy's lonely death.

'That's the saddest story I ever heard,' said Frankie, and Alice nodded wordlessly in agreement.

'O.K. so he wasn't a deliberate sacrifice,' said Dog Boy. 'But he was still a little boy who died in the dunes.' He watched as two children ran past, kicking up sand. 'And I don't know how to stop it happening again.'

'I'm really scared, now,' said Alice. 'My twin

brothers are having a birthday party down here tomorrow, with all their friends.'

'Can't you suggest something else instead?' asked Dog Boy.

Alice shook her head and her eyes glistened with tears. 'They've done nothing else but talk about it all week. I'm supposed to be coming too, to help my mum with the games and tea and stuff.'

'Then we'll all come,' said David decisively. 'We'll all come and we'll stand guard. We'll watch them so closely they won't have a chance to get into danger. Agreed?'

Frankie, Michael and Dog Boy looked at one another and nodded their heads. 'Agreed,' they said.

9

'It's so good of all your friends to come and help,' said Alice's mum, staggering across the sand clutching a huge picnic hamper.

'They wanted to,' said Alice, shortly, watching as Frankie and David caught two of the party boys and herded them back to the main group. They had managed to keep everyone together all the way from the car park, through the dunes and on to the beach. They were not about to let them escape now.

'Are you sure they wanted to?' Mrs Mitchell stopped and gave Alice a searching look.

'What do you mean?' said Alice.

'It's just that, they're all taking it so – seriously. Especially your new friend. What was his name . . .?'

'Dog Boy,' muttered Alice.

'Yes . . . Dog Boy,' said Mrs Mitchell, frowning in a puzzled way at the tall young man with his hair in dreadlocks who was striding along behind the twins like a jailer escorting his prisoners. She dumped the picnic hamper on the sand. 'Here, I think. Don't you?' she said and started spreading rugs.

'What about a bit further along?' suggested Alice, glancing uneasily at the dunes behind her. They were still very close to the dune where the boy was buried.

'No, this will be fine,' said Mrs Mitchell. 'There's too much to carry far. Hand me the bag of presents, will you?'

'But, Dad might not be able to find us here,' said Alice.

'Yes he will,' said Mrs Mitchell. She opened the lid of the hamper and two helium-filled balloons popped out. The balloons were tied to the handles of the hamper and they stopped short just above Alice's head, tugging gently on their strings. 'See?' said Mrs Mitchell. 'Marker buoys. Your dad can't miss us and the boys can go off where they like without worrying about getting lost.'

'I don't think that's such a good idea,' said Alice.

'Alice!' said Mrs Mitchell with more than a hint of exasperation. 'Just put the presents on the rug, will you?'

Alice sighed and emptied the presents out of the hold-all onto the rug. Her own presents to the twins were still in her pockets along with two boxes of birthday candles and a box of matches. She had bought them each a little Star Wars fighter made out of chocolate, with their names written in icing on the side. Alice reached into her pocket to add them to the pile, then changed her mind. She decided to save them for later, when all this was over and the twins were safely back at home.

'Presents!' called Mrs Mitchell and the twins and their friends turned and headed for the rug like ten heat-seeking missiles. Alice barely got out of the way in time.

'They don't muck about, do they?' said David as they watched chunks of torn wrapping paper flying into the air. 'It's like a feeding frenzy.'

'At least they're all in one place for a while,' sighed Frankie, collapsing onto the sand.

'That's an extra one from Mum and Dad,' said Alice, leaning forward to get a better view as Gary and Kevin tore the wrapping from a long, thin parcel with a lump on the end. 'It was a last minute request. Mum nipped out late yesterday afternoon to get it.'

The twins jumped up triumphantly and brandished the last minute present over their heads. Gary was waving a pair of headphones and Kevin was holding some sort of a long, thin tube with a disc attached to one end.

'What is that?' said Michael. 'It looks like a frisbee on a stick.'

'Oh, no,' said Frankie softly as she realised what it was. 'That's a metal detector.'

They had time to share one, horrified glance before the twins and their friends raced off towards the dunes to try out their new toy. The three dogs ran merrily alongside.

'Quick!' yelled Alice. 'Follow them!'

'Now just a minute,' said Mrs Mitchell. 'You let them go, do you hear? You can't keep following them around all afternoon. I won't allow it.'

'But—' said Alice.

'No buts! If you all really want to help, then you can clear up this wrapping paper, pack away the other presents and set out the food.'

Alice was about to argue, but Dog Boy shook his head. 'You stay. I'll go,' he whispered. 'I'll keep them

116

away from the dune. Just going to get my dogs!' he called to Mrs Mitchell, then he sprinted off after the party boys.

'Right,' said Mrs Mitchell, folding her arms and giving them a stern look. 'To work.' She looked up at the horizon where a bank of dark cloud was growing. 'And quickly, please. I have a feeling this party is going to be over sooner than we planned.'

'What made them ask for a metal detector?' asked Alice as she set out paper plates around the edges of the rugs. The wind was getting stronger and she was having to weight each plate with a peanut butter sandwich.

'It's all your fault, actually,' said Mrs Mitchell, lifting the cake from the hamper and placing it carefully in the middle of the rugs. 'Gary and Kevin were telling me all about you lot digging for treasure in the dunes.'

'But we weren't!'

'Well, you know those two. Strong imaginations. Anyway, they said they wanted to treasure hunt too – on their birthday. It's a good job I went out to the shop when I did. That was the last one. The man said there'd been quite a run on them. Holiday-makers, I suppose.'

Mrs Mitchell carried on setting out chocolate biscuits and fairy cakes, humming the happy birthday tune under her breath. She did not notice the look of horrified understanding passing between the four friends. The twins were chatterboxes, everybody knew that. If the twins had told Mrs Mitchell about treasure in the dunes, the chances were they had told other people as well, and the treasure would have grown with every telling.

Quietly, they dropped what they were doing and turned to scan the dunes.

'Yes, there they are,' said David, softly, watching sunlight glinting off the metal detectors which moved amongst the dips and hollows. 'We didn't notice them before, we were too busy watching the kids, but they're there all right.'

'There's Nigel and his mates,' said Frankie staring at a little group of distant figures moving across the skyline with black headphones clamped to their ears.

'And look!' said Michael, pointing out a taller couple with a detector and a spade between them. 'That's James Nardini and Miss Broadbent!'

'What are we going to do?' asked Alice, her voice shrill with barely controlled panic.

'I'm going to go and talk to her,' said David. 'Warn her off, somehow. Are you coming?'

Alice glanced back at her mother, then over toward the dunes where Dog Boy had taken the twins, trying to decide where she should be. Finally, she nodded at David and they all moved off together, heading towards Miss Broadbent. Just then, the growing bank of storm clouds finally reached the sun and blotted it out. Instantly, the wind moved into a higher gear.

'Hey!' called Mrs Mitchell, looking up as all the paper plates dumped their sandwich weights into the sand and went flapping away along the beach. A corner of the rug snapped in the wind, flicking a pebble-dash of sand over the birthday cake. The next blast of wind snapped the balloon strings and the two balloons went spiralling away into the darkening sky.

'Alice!' called Mrs Mitchell, struggling to get the cake back into the hamper. 'Alice! Come back and help!'

But Alice didn't turn back. The wind was whipping her long, black hair around her ears, making it difficult to hear anything and her mother's shouts sounded like the cries of a distant gull. The four of them had reached the dunes and were struggling to climb up to Miss Broadbent against the rising force of the wind.

'Miss!' called David, cupping his hands around his mouth. Miss Broadbent turned, hesitated, then left James Nardini and hurried down the slope to meet them.

'Miss!' yelled David. 'You should go home. Now!'

'It's O.K.' smiled Miss Broadbent. 'It's only a bit of wind.'

'No, I mean it's dangerous to dig in the dunes, Miss.'

Miss Broadbent's smile disappeared. 'Oh, I see,' she said. 'Are we getting too close, is that it?'

'Pardon, Miss?'

'Are Mr Nardini and I getting too close to your little treasure hoard?'

David tried again. 'Miss, we did find something in the dunes, but it wasn't gold. Really, Miss, you should leave now, for your own safety.'

Miss Broadbent's pretty face hardened. 'Do you really think I want to spend the rest of my life teaching history to kids like you?'

David took a step back. He looked as though Miss

Broadbent had just reached out and slapped him in the face. The teacher stared at him for a second, then shrugged her shoulders. 'I'm sorry, David,' she said, turning away and climbing back up the slope towards James Nardini. 'Now go away, we're busy.'

Frankie glared at the teacher's retreating back. 'Read my lips. There is no gold, stupid!' she yelled. 'And you're not so pretty either. Your butt looks enormous in those trousers, lady! What?' she said, seeing Michael's shocked face. 'I don't care. I'm not around next term.'

'Come on,' said David, heading away across the slope of the dune.

'Where to?' asked Alice, running to catch up.

'No-one's going to listen,' said David. 'We can't make them leave. So we'll have to stand guard over the box. At least we can make sure nobody digs in that hollow.'

They trudged in a straggling line along the top of the dunes, holding their arms up to protect their eyes as the wind flung stinging needles of sand into their faces.

'Look,' shouted Michael, pointing down to the nearly deserted beach where Mrs Mitchell was still struggling to fold the picnic rugs. A cluster of little boys stood watching her, looking tiny and vulnerable as the wind flattened their bright summer shorts against their legs. Alice counted heads and her heart sank as she realised that only eight boys had returned. The twins were nowhere in sight and neither was Dog Boy. She suddenly had an awful feeling that the twins were already in the dune hollow, prising open the top of the strange stone box they had found to see what was inside.

Alice broke into a run, stretching her long legs. She left the others behind and ploughed ahead through the soft sand, pushing herself on until she thought her lungs would burst.

Please, please, please, she thought as the rim of the hollow came in sight. *Please don't let them be down there.* She flung herself up the last part of the slope and landed on her belly with her head hanging over the lip of the hollow. There was no-one there.

Alice let out one relieved sob, then she rolled over onto her back and lay there, pulling deep breaths of air into her hurting lungs. First David, then Frankie, then Michael caught up and collapsed onto the sand beside her to recover. Finally, Alice sat up again and scanned the beach, trying to spot the twins.

'Oh, no,' she said, softly, staring at a small group of people struggling over the dunes towards them. As she watched, James Nardini spotted her and stopped, pointing her out to the others. Miss Broadbent was beside him and Nigel and his friends were trailing along behind.

'What is it?' said David, sitting up next to her.

'They're following us,' said Alice. 'They must think we're going to lead them to the gold.'

'Right,' said David. 'Battle stations. Whatever happens, we have to stop them digging here.' He hurried down into the hollow, followed by Alice and Michael.

Frankie clambered to her feet with a tired groan. 'There is no gold!' she yelled into the wind, but the little group kept moving towards them. 'Some people won't be told,' she sighed and headed down the slope to join the others. As she reached the bottom of the slope, fat drops of rain started to fall, making little craters in the sand. The rain grew heavier until it was pouring into the hollow in a solid sheet. Then lightning flashed overhead and a deep rumble shook the ground. Miss Broadbent's storm had finally arrived.

'O.K.' gasped Frankie, stumbling over to the others. 'O.K. I'm wet. I'm wet and I'm mad! What are we supposed to do now?'

'Keep our fingers crossed,' said David. 'The box is hidden. There's no reason why they should find it.'

They huddled together, waiting for the treasure hunters to appear at the top of the hollow. Thunder cracked again and the rain battered down on their heads, running in little rivers down their necks. David glanced anxiously at the slope where the box was buried and saw that the sand was slowly trickling away, slipping to the bottom of the slope in wet runnels.

Alice and David tried to push more sand over the box, but it was washed away as soon as they patted it into place. Then the broken front slab fell away from the box, narrowly missing Michael as it fell.

Alice raised her hands to David in a gesture of defeat but David would not give up. He manhandled them all into a line in front of the box, then turned and waited, glaring up at the top of the dune with his fists clenched.

'Perhaps the storm has sent them packing,' yelled Michael, looking at David.

David shook his head and pointed up to the top of

the dune. First one figure, then a second, then three or four others appeared. They stood on the rim of the hollow, black shapes against the darkening sky, clutching their metal detectors and their spades.

'Here we go,' muttered Frankie, swiping the water from her face.

James Nardini took a step into the hollow.

And then everything changed.

The air shimmered and suddenly the bedraggled group of treasure hunters were no longer there. In their place stood half a dozen tough, muscled men dressed in breeches and belted, knee-length tunics. They wore woollen cloaks slung round their shoulders, held in place by large, metal brooches. The spades and metal detectors had been replaced with long, wooden shields, broad-bladed iron daggers and slender spears, which the men carried with comfortable familiarity.

'They're not real,' said David, in a voice that very nearly managed to be steady. 'They can't hurt us.'

One of the men hefted a spear with casual ease and sent it arrowing down into the hollow. It embedded itself a foot deep in the sand at David's feet. Frankie screamed and Michael clutched at Alice's hand. The man who threw the spear turned his back on them to talk to his companions and they all saw the thick, bleached plait of hair at the nape of his neck.

Slowly, Alice leaned forward and gazed at the spear. It was still vibrating from the impact and the raindrops on its smooth surface quivered in time to the vibrations.

'It's real,' she whispered to David. 'It could have killed one of us.'

She reached forward to touch the spear and there was an angry yell from the top of the dune. A second spear thudded into the ground beside the first and Alice jumped back. The lead warrior was glaring at her with eyes like chips of blue ice.

'Stay absolutely still,' said David, under his breath.

'But they're going to come down here and – they're going to make us into slaves, or they might even—' Frankie choked on her words and began to cry softly as the men started to spread out around the rim of the hollow, blocking them in.

'Oh! I see!' said Michael, suddenly. He turned his head to look into the stone box behind them. 'It's him,' he said, softly, staring in at the face of the little boy. 'He's the one. He's doing it.'

'The boy?' said Alice, trying to watch all six men at once. 'The thing in the dunes – it's the boy?'

'Yes. He's blindsiding us. Remember, Frankie?'

Frankie wiped the tears and rain from her face. 'Everybody's heart's got a blind side. How big your blind side is depends on what sort of a shape your heart's been knocked into,' she intoned, like a child repeating a nursery rhyme.

'And the blind side of his heart must be ginormous!' said Michael. 'Think of the shape it's been knocked into. He died thinking his dad had abandoned him. He died alone and angry. Dog Boy told us the Celts believed the spirit of a dead person could turn nasty if it was neglected. Well that's just what he's done. Everyone's an enemy, to him.'

'That's why it's always little boys who die. Boys the same age as him,' said Alice. 'He must be so jealous of them, running around the dunes, all full of life.'

'We haven't got time for this,' muttered David, watching the men. 'We need to do something.'

'If we could just appease him, somehow,' said Michael. 'Make him feel better.'

'And how do we do that?'

'I don't know,' admitted Michael.

They drew together and held hands, waiting for the warriors to come down and finish them. Michael closed his eyes and Frankie began to cry again. Alice thought about her family. She thought about Gary and Kevin and the way her mum soothed them when they got upset and tired – and suddenly, she knew exactly what to do.

Gritting her teeth, Alice turned her back on the warriors and kneeled down in the sand. 'Hello,' she said to the boy curled inside the box. 'I got you something.' Digging her hand into her pocket, she pulled out the two chocolate Star Wars fighters and laid them in the box at the boy's feet. 'That's good chocolate,' she said, attempting a wobbly smile. 'Expensive.'

She glanced behind her. The warriors were still standing on the rim of the hollow, taking their time. Turning back, she wiped her wet hands on the inside of her jacket and dug into her pocket again, bringing out the birthday candles and matches. Leaning into the box, she quickly stuck all the birthday candles into the pile of salt next to the chocolate fighters. 'I want you to know something,' she said, as she fumbled some matches out of the box. 'I want you to know that your father loved you.'

Thunder cracked directly overhead and she nearly dropped the matches. 'You were his most precious thing. He tried to come back, he really did.' Alice struck a match and held it to each of the candles until they were all burning with little flames like stars, lighting up the inside of the box that had been full of darkness for two thousand years. Outside the box the rain still drummed down onto the sand and the wind howled, but inside it was dry and peaceful.

'I'll tell you something else, too,' said Alice, smiling for real this time as she gazed in at the little wizened face. 'Your father would have been proud of you. You were such a good little boy and so brave – and you did exactly what he told you to do, didn't you? You looked after his dagger for him and you protected yourself whenever anyone came close to finding you.'

Alice took a deep breath, then pushed her arm into the box and gently cupped the side of the little boy's head with her hand. 'But, sweetheart, it's time to go to sleep now. You're very tired, aren't you?' she said, looking at his drooping lids and the soft curve of his eyelashes. 'Shhh, now.' She stroked his papery forehead lightly with her fingers and a drop of rain water fell from the sleeve of her jacket onto his face, running down his cheek like a tear.

'Ssshhh. It's all right. Go to sleep, sweetheart. That's it.'

The little body shifted slightly, slumping over to rest against the side wall of the box. 'Good boy,' whispered Alice. 'Night night. I'll leave the lights on.'

Slowly, Alice pulled her arm out of the box and stood up. Another earth-shaking rumble filled the hollow and it took her a second to realise that this time, it wasn't thunder. She looked up and saw the whole side of the dune above her beginning to shift.

'Run!' she shrieked.

They pelted over to the other side of the hollow and flattened themselves against the face of the dune. There was a heavy whump behind them and the floor of the hollow shook. Then the rain and the wind stopped and there was a moment of absolute quiet. Alice raised her head and looked behind her. The box had completely disappeared, buried under tons of sand.

'Is it over?' asked Frankie, climbing cautiously to her feet.

'It's over,' said Alice, and her voice was thick with tears.

Someone ran down into the hollow and David jumped to his feet, preparing to fight. But it was not a man with a broad bladed dagger standing in front of him. It was Miss Broadbent and she was gazing at him in confusion. She put her hand to the side of her head and stared around the hollow as though she was not quite sure how she had got there. Her wet hair hung in dripping rats tails and the purpling bruise round her eye stood out in sharp contrast to her white face.

'Are you all right, David?' she said. 'The whole side of the dune just collapsed. You could have been hurt!'

'I'm fine,' said David, shortly. 'And you're too busy looking for treasure to worry about kids like me, remember?'

'Did I say that? I did, didn't I?' Miss Broadbent rubbed her face with her hands and then sent a

127

confused glance up at the silhouetted figure of James Nardini. She frowned. 'I – don't know what came over me, David. Gold fever, I suppose. I didn't mean what I said. I love teaching.'

'Right.' David gave Miss Broadbent a hard little smile, then turned his back on her.

The teacher shook her head, then floundered up the slope to James Nardini. She tugged at his arm, urging him to go with her, but he pulled out of her grip and gazed down at the four bedraggled figures in the bottom of the hollow with an expression of greedy anger. Miss Broadbent slipped away, heading for town, but he did not notice. Frankie folded her arms and glared back at him. For a long moment their gazes locked.

'Read my lips!' shouted Frankie, suddenly. 'There. Is. No. Gold!'

James Nardini scowled at her then turned and hurried after Miss Broadbent.

'Too late!' yelled Frankie. 'You've lost her now!'

She turned to grin at Michael, but he was staring up at the remaining treasure hunters. One of the silhouetted figures standing at the top of the dune looked familiar to him.

'Dad?' he whispered and a spasm of pain crossed his face. His father was one of the treasure hunters, carrying a metal detector in his hand. He watched as Mr Adams hurried down the slope towards him, holding out the metal detector. Michael was about to turn away in disgust when he saw that it was not a metal detector at all, but a tightly furled umbrella.

'I thought you might need this,' said Mr Adams,

peering at Michael from under the hood of his waterproof and holding out the umbrella.

Michael's face softened with surprise. He took the umbrella and stood there, waiting for the catch, but Mr Adams simply nodded, then turned on his heel and walked off again. Michael blinked and then he smiled.

'Thanks!' he called up to the retreating figure. 'Thanks, Dad! Did you see?' he said, turning to Frankie. 'He brought me an umbrella!'

'Nice,' said Frankie. 'I'm pleased for you. Really I am.'

They climbed out of the hollow just as the sun broke through the clouds. Alice scanned the dunes and smiled with relief as she spotted Dog Boy and the twins waving from the car park. She waved back madly, jumping up and down.

'I'd better go and find Mum,' she said to Frankie. 'Tell her the twins are safe and waiting by the car.'

'Um, you don't need to go find her,' said Frankie. 'She's on her way.'

They watched as Mrs Mitchell clambered towards them from the beach with eight little boys trailing along behind her.

'Uh oh,' said Frankie, catching sight of her face. 'She looks real mad. I think I'll just go and see Dog Boy.'

'Me too,' said Alice, hurriedly, retreating towards the car park.

'Alice Mitchell!' called a thunderous voice, stopping her in her tracks. 'Don't you dare run off again! I want a word with you!'

10

Alice struck the match and cupped her hand round it until she was sure the flame would burn strongly, then she leaned forward and began to light the candles, holding her hair back with her other hand. The tip of her tongue poked from the corner of her mouth as she concentrated on touching the flame to all eight candles before the match burned down.

'There,' she said, softly, sitting back on her heels in the sand.

'Happy Birthday to you,' began Mrs Mitchell, waving her arms like a conductor to encourage everyone else to join in. 'Happy Birthday to you!'

The Birthday song rose into the hot summer air and the twins went red in the face and punched each other on the arm. Alice smiled at them affectionately and they pulled horrible faces at her. She shook her head and let her gaze travel around the circle of singers. Her dad was next to her mum with his arm round her shoulders, belting out the song for all he was worth. Next to him, Mr Adams stood stiffly, mouthing the words through lips which hardly moved and casting disdainful glances at Dog Boy on his right.

Well, it's a start, thought Alice, looking over at Michael, who was watching his father out of the corner of his eye, his face a mixture of wariness and hope.

Alice looked back to Dog Boy. He had spotted the twins making horrible faces at all the singers and he was gurning back at them with great enthusiasm. Alice thought about the day after the storm, when the four of them had gone to visit him in his van. They had told him the story of the boy in the dunes and Dog Boy had cried a little, then he had pulled his fact file out of the drawer and dumped it in the bin. Watching him now, Alice thought he might be moving on soon.

As the song came to an end, she looked over at her friends. Michael gave her a gentle smile, David winked and Frankie did a wickedly brilliant impression of Mr Adams trying to sing. Alice giggled.

'Make a wish!' ordered Mrs Mitchell as the twins surged forward to blow out the candles. They both stopped dead and shut their eyes, screwing up their faces in concentration. There was an instant of stillness. Alice looked at the pale candle flames fluttering in the breeze, then she gazed over to the dunes, where another little boy had finally fallen asleep. A lump came to her throat.

The twins filled their cheeks with air, then blasted the candles out. Everybody clapped and Mrs Mitchell cut the cake into generous wedges. Alice, David, Frankie and Michael each took a piece and wandered off down the beach together.

'Hang on!' called Dog Boy from behind them.

They turned and waited as he sprinted towards them, with Daisy, Clem and Jet dancing at his heels.

'So . . . Nice party,' he said, when he had caught up with them.

'Yeah,' said Frankie, looking at him curiously. He looked different somehow. He was smiling, and the smile fitted his face well, lighting up his green and blue eyes and showing off his white teeth. 'What's up?'

'Nothing much,' said Dog Boy, ducking to pick up a stick for the dogs. He threw it in a high curve and the dogs tore off up the beach after it. 'Just wanted to say thanks,' he said, staring after the dogs. 'For solving the mystery. It can't help Andrew, but it helps me. Knowing.' He shrugged. 'I can't explain why.'

'It's important,' said Michael simply, and Dog Boy shot him a grateful smile.

'Where are you going to go now?' asked Alice.

Dog Boy turned to look at her with a surprised expression, then his smile returned and he gave her a nod of respect. 'Thought I'd head North,' he said. 'Join some friends campaigning against a new ski development in the Highlands.'

David frowned. 'People need jobs,' he began, but stopped when Frankie gave him a look.

Dog Boy laughed then held out his hand to David. 'It's Alex,' he said. 'My name. You wanted to know.'

David grinned and shook his hand. 'Goodbye, Alex,' he said.

Dog Boy turned and headed off up the beach after his dogs, lifting his arm in a wave without looking back. They watched until he disappeared into the dunes, then continued their stroll.

'It's just an ordinary beach now, isn't it?' said Michael, licking the icing from his fingers.

'Yes,' said Alice, adjusting the strap of her swimming costume and tilting her face to the sun.

'You did a good job there, Alice.'

'I know,' said Alice, smiling smugly.

They moved down to the edge of the sea and splashed on through the shallow water, finishing their cake in a companionable silence.

'Your mom seems to have forgiven you for abandoning her on Sunday,' said Frankie, after a while, bending to wash her sticky hands in the water.

'Huh!' said Alice, turning to gaze back at her mum, who was trying to persuade ten little boys to lie down for a game of sleeping lions. 'Only because I spent the last three days doing hard labour. I had to make the whole picnic again. Cake and everything.'

'You made the cake?' said David with an expression of mock horror on his face. 'But I just ate some!'

'Shut up,' said Alice. She pushed him right in the middle of his chest and he overbalanced and fell backwards into the sea.

'Neat!' giggled Frankie. Alice smiled over at her, then gasped with shock as a pair of cold, wet hands grabbed her ankles. The hands yanked and Alice went down into the freezing water.

Frankie slipped her little rucksack from her shoulders and placed it carefully on the sand higher up the beach, then she turned and raced back down to the sea.

'Geronimo!' she yelled, launching herself into the waves.

Michael waded in slowly as the others splashed and played around him. Frankie's wet curls sparkled, Alice's hair floated out behind her like seaweed and David dived and swam, as sleek as a seal. Michael smiled, pinched his nose and lowered himself carefully into the sea.

They swam until they were tired, then Frankie collected her rucksack and they made their way to a large flat rock at the edge of the sea. They stretched out on the sun-warmed stone and let the breeze dry them.

'Got you a present,' said Frankie, nudging Alice in the ribs.

Alice opened her eyes and peered up at Frankie, squinting against the sun. 'What is it?'

'Duh!' said Frankie. 'You won't know that until you open it.'

Alice sat up as Frankie pulled a soft, flat parcel from her rucksack. David and Michael turned to watch as Alice tore open the wrapping.

'Oh,' she said, staring down at the grey material inside. 'It's a school skirt.'

'Say thank you,' said Frankie, bouncing up and down with barely suppressed excitement.

'Thank you,' said Alice, automatically. 'But, why?'

'Because I'm gonna need mine after all,' grinned Frankie.

Alice gave Frankie a bewildered frown, then her face brightened with sudden understanding. 'You're staying!' she yelled.

'I'm staying!' Frankie yelled back.

'Oh, Frankie, that's wonderful!' said Alice, leaning over to hug her friend.

Michael said nothing, just nodded his head vigorously and beamed at Frankie.

'Great,' said David, trying to stop grinning. 'Another year of hassle. Just when I was looking forward to a peaceful time.'

'But, it was definite, you said. You were going. What changed?' asked Alice.

Frankie wriggled with excitement. 'Well, you know I told you how my mom barfed up in the sink on the day she arrived?'

'Yeah . . .'

'And I thought it was travel sickness?'

'Yeah . . .'

'I was wrong. My mom was still barfing up this morning,' grinned Frankie.

'What's so funny about that?' said Alice.

'She's barfing up because she's going to have a baby,' said Frankie, hugging herself delightedly. 'They're both a bit surprised, I think, but happy-surprised. So, anyway, we're staying! They've decided. Mom's having the baby here, Dad's taking that second twelve-month contract with the oil company. What can I say – you ain't getting rid of me yet.'

Frankie grinned at them all then rearranged her face into a serious expression. 'There's only one problem,' she said.

'What?' said Michael, anxiously.

Frankie sighed. 'I have to go back to school next term and face Big Butt Broadbent after all.'

There was a surprised silence, then Alice, David and Michael all burst out laughing. Soon they were laughing so hard, they were rolling around and beating the rock with their fists.

'Big butt . . .' gasped David, between howls of laughter.

'You're not so pretty, lady,' mimicked Michael, setting them off again.

'Stop,' squawked Alice, flapping her hands weakly. 'I can't take any more!'

Frankie grinned wickedly and leaned toward Alice. 'Hey, lady, did you know your butt looks enormous in those trousers?'

'No,' squeaked Alice as tears of laughter rolled down her cheeks.

'Big butt. Massive butt. Butt the size of Alaska,' chanted Frankie.

Alice drummed her heels on the rock and dislodged Frankie's present.

They leaned together, laughing, and nobody noticed as Alice's fourth new school skirt of the year slipped off the rock and into the sea. It floated there for a few seconds, slowly darkening as the water soaked into it, then it sank under the waves and was gone.